<u>**Snow In November – LeAnne Keely**</u>

Published by Ink And Quill Press, 2025

For more excellent works of fiction, visit Inkandquillpress.com

Cover artwork by LeAnne Withrow

Chapter One

Helen stole a nervous glance at her passenger.

Luciana was flipping through a book and looking effortlessly beautiful. The sun, shining in through the passenger side window of Helen's tiny sedan, hit Luciana's dark hair, making it shine almost as bright as her eyes did—even now, buried in hundred-year-old fiction.

Not just any fiction either, an *original* copy of The Hobbit.

Luciana had one arm propped against the window sill, her hand up and supporting her perfect cheekbones as she leaned against it while the other gently held the timeworn novel. She was wearing a pair of golden hoop earrings, a thin gold necklace, and a number of rings—all of which set off the warmth in her skin tone delightfully and contrasted sharply with the deep crimson of her v-necked, sleeveless top and khaki shorts.

It should *almost* be a crime to wear pants when you had legs like that, Helen caught herself thinking as she drank in the sight of chiseled calves and full, firm thighs.

The sudden crunch of gravel had her jerking her eyes back to the highway in time to yank the wheel—a little too forcefully—to get them back in their lane and off the shoulder.

Helen felt her face go as red as her passenger's top and sank a little lower in her seat. She could feel Luciana's eye probing her but refused to turn.

"You ok?"

Luciana's hand brushed her shoulder, sending a shiver of excitement down Helen's spine, shooting out along her nerves like lightning.

"Yeah," she laughed nervously. "I was just, y'know, daydreaming."

"Do you need a break? Is something–"

"No, I've just never driven with someone so distracting in my car before," Helen's eyes went wide and she gulped. "Not that you're a problem, or that you're *too* distracting. I mean, I *can* drive; I've had people in my–I'm gonna stop talking now."

She trailed off, biting her lip to keep from blurting anything else out.

Get it together, Helen.

Luciana's laughter was, thankfully, sweet and warm—and completely empty of any mockery or malice.

"If it helps," she said, dropping a hand to Helen's lap and squeezing her thigh. "I've never *ridden* in a car with someone so distracting either."

Helen tried to ignore the heat building between her legs and in her chest.

Luciana must've sensed Helen's struggle because, after a quick peck on the cheek, she returned to her book.

Helen looked over just in time to see the page of the woman's novel turn itself, then focused back on the road.

"Damn, that would be convenient."

"Hmm?"

"Not having to turn your own pages."

"Ah, well," Luciana's cheeks went a bit pink. "I don't do it all the time, I'm just really comfortable in this position."

"Hey, no shade from me," Helen smiled. "I'd do it if I could."

"Shade?"

"It means...it means, no judgment. Kinda."

"Got it, thanks."

They fell back into silence as Luciana was re-engrossed by her book and Helen put her mind back to the task at hand. They were in Kansas now, crossing the nigh-endless fields of sunflowers and wheat that marked one of Helen's least favorite states.

But Luciana was calling the shots as far as where they were headed, and Helen didn't mind. She wasn't sure where *exactly* their destination was, but Luciana had mentioned wanting to head out west to Colorado, so she figured her best bet was to hop up to 70 West and go from there.

An old David Allan Coe song came on the radio, and Helen turned the volume dial up a few notches as she caught the tune and hummed along.

Annoying as always.

"Oh shit, hey do you mind if I sing, sorry."

"I was hoping you would," Luciana answered warmly, not looking up from her book. "You have a lovely voice."

Helen blushed and couldn't help but smile. Before long, she was humming again. Humming turned to singing, and singing turned to belting as they cruised north, and Helen lost herself in the moment.

The state might be blank as hell, but at least the tunes were good.

"So, I guess we're *UHauling*," Helen nudged her passenger playfully a few hours later. "Check that off the bucket list."

"What?"

Helen glanced over, her smile faltering.

"Y-y'know, UHauling," she searched Luciana's eyes and found nothing but genuine curiosity. "It's, um, well, it's a stereotype about lesbians these days. That we move quickly—that we uh, move in together or run off together right away."

Her words trailed off awkwardly and she turned back to the empty highway.

"So then, do you identify as a lesbian?"

Helen choked on air and struggled through a coughing fit before croaking out an answer.

"No," she stammered. "Well, I mean *yes,* but not like a gold star or anything. I mean, I think of myself as a lesbian, but I've been with a few guys too, or whatever."

"Gold star?"

"Yeah, it's this stupid thing," Helen said, running a hand through her hair. "Like 'never been with a man' lesbians are better or different somehow from other lesbians? It's kinda toxic, honestly."

"Ah."

"N-not that there's anything wrong with that either, if you're–"

"I'm not," Luciana placated her with a smile. "I agree with you, that seems…toxic. Though I don't think of myself as…well, anything honestly. I've lived my life believing that connections can happen with anyone."

"Hearts not parts," Helen smiled warmly.

"Cute," Luciana chuckled before turning wistfully toward the window. "Language has changed so much since I was last...out and about. I'm guessing I have a lot of other things to catch up on too."

"Yeah," Helen frowned subconsciously. "God, there's actually a *ton* of stuff, and I'm hardly qualified to teach–"

"Helen, relax."

She tried, she really did, but the new and building tension in her jaw and shoulders seemed determined to stick around.

"What's wrong?"

Helen tried to hide behind a warm smile, but she could tell from Luciana's quirked eyebrow that she wasn't fooling her.

"You make me nervous," she blurted out. "I'm not totally sure where we stand after our…fight. I don't know what to do, where to go, or anything except…except that I want to be where you are."

"Helen, we don't have to *stand* anywhere," she shrugged, an unusual gesture for the normally poised woman. "I am glad you came back—very glad—but I have no intention of dismissing the feelings that led you to leave, and I don't think pressuring you is the right thing to do either. Figure out where your head and your heart are, and I'll meet you there."

Is this what butterflies feel like?

"Besides, the unknown is always a bit frightening," her lover said, turning to look out the window at the landscape speeding past. "But I can answer at least part of that for you. We are going to visit an old friend of mine in Colorado, he can give me the…lay of the land, so to speak."

An old friend?

Helen felt a pang of jealousy, then stamped it down as best she could.

"Is this old friend Fae, like you?"

"Yes, older in fact. He keeps to himself mostly, or at least he used to."

"Why don't we just, you know," Helen snapped her fingers dramatically. "Poof our way there?"

Luciana laughed, and Helen felt herself smiling in response. God, the woman was intoxicating.

"Unfortunately, I am not quite as powerful out here in the world as I was within my own domain," she shrugged. "And, until I know who is doing what and where, it's best to be a bit more unobtrusive than that."

Helen nodded, considering the implications of Luciana's statement. She opened her mouth to ask a question but was interrupted by the shrill ring of her cellphone. She recognized the air raid siren ringtone—it was the only custom one she'd set up—as belonging to her mother.

She flicked her eyes toward Luciana, who was already looking at her.

"Do you need some privacy?"

"No," Helen gulped, shaking her head. "I'd rather have you with me for this."

She reached out a hand and tapped the call accept button on her dashboard display, quieting the device with a click.

Silence.

Helen could feel her palms growing clammy, and she licked her lips to fight the sudden dryness in her mouth.

"Oh, honestly, Helen," her mother's voice fairly dripped with irritation. "I can *hear* that you're driving."

"S-sorry," she glanced skyward in frustration. "Sorry, Mom, I was–"

"And stop apologizing so much; it's unbecoming."

"Sorry."

"When will you be home? It's ten hours from Oklahoma City, so you should be well into Tennessee by now."

"Well, actually, I'm–"

"Of course, here it comes," Helen flinched at her mother's tone. "What now, Helen? Did you 'total your car' in a river again?"

"Mom, I *did* get in that wreck, I told you," Helen felt her voice rising. "And no, it's just that–"

"Helen–"

"I'm not coming home," Helen shouted. "Not right now, I mean."

Silence.

"Sorry, I…I've got some things to do," she added more quietly.

"So you're going on another bender, is that it?"

Helen looked over at Luciana, but the woman's poker face was immaculate.

"I'm not going on a bender, mom," she hissed back.

"Where will your not-bender be taking place? Arkansas? Missouri?"

"I'm going to Colorado–"

"You understand, of course, that that is the *opposite* direction from Tennessee."

"Yes," Helen ground her teeth.

"I wish I knew why you enjoyed putting me through this, Helen, I really do," her mother's waspish voice grated her nerves like sharpened blades. "I *knew* I should've listened to your psychiatrist and kept you here."

"Sorry, Mom."

"If you were *sorry,* you wouldn't be going to Colorado," the woman jabbed. "You should be home so that *someone* can make sure you're taking your pills and going to your appointments, God knows you're not doing it on your own."

"Mom!"

"You think I can't tell? When's the last time you took–"

"Goodbye, Mom, I love you."

Helen clicked her dashboard again, hanging up the call in the middle of her mother's sentence. She watched her hand curl into a white-knuckled fist and fought the desire to punch something.

"I'm sorry that you carry this…burden," Luciana's soft words drew Helen's eyes.

The woman was half-turned in her direction, her book closed and sitting in her lap, and her hands clasped.

"I sometimes forget that human relationships are just as volatile as those of my kind."

"Do you get along with your parents?"

"Well, it isn't exactly like that. Do you recall how I told you most of our kind don't have children?"

"Mhmm," Helen nodded, switching lanes to pass the first car they'd seen in twenty minutes but listening closely.

"My sister and I were exceptions. We were born about forty years apart—a very short time considering most Fae—and raised by our three mothers until we were old enough to be on our own."

"And now?"

"Fae don't really keep those kinds of ties," she sighed. "Though I often wish we did."

"You don't see your family, ever?"

"Not in a very long time."

"But you miss them?"

"I miss my sister," Luciana shrugged again. "Very few Fae have them, and we shared a really strong bond until…"

"Until you stopped going out?"

"Yes."

"I'm sorry, I'm not trying to bring up anything painful."

Luciana's laugh was a surprise, but the spreading warmth in Helen's chest drew a smile to her lips.

"What?"

"You're just very kind."

Helen's cheeks burned red in the afternoon light and she adjusted in her seat.

"Ok, my turn to cheer you up, when's the last time you were out and about, approximately?"

"August, 1969, for about a week."

"Ok…so you know we landed on the moon right?"

"Yes," Luciana burst out laughing. "I recall following the Space Race quite closely on the radio."

"On the radio," Helen shook her head in disbelief. "That's just wild."

"*Woodstock* was wild," Luciana countered.

"Holy shit, you were at Woodstock?"

"Yep," Luciana's gaze grew distant. "A lot of us went, actually. I'd known Jimi for a few centuries at that point, and with all of the–"

"Hold on," Helen's mind was reeling. "Jimi *Hendrix*? Jimi Hendrix was Fae?"

"Of course, you think a mortal man could play like that?"

"That's a surprisingly good point," Helen scratched her chin.

"But that was it. After Woodstock I knew I had made a mistake—knew I had to go back to Casa De Rosas."

"Why?"

"He showed up, The Smiling Man."

"Oh," Helen felt her brow furrowing. "You said you weren't as powerful now, that we had to lay low. Is that because of him?"

"Yes," the woman nodded. "I'm sure he's grown more powerful since then, and I couldn't defeat him before so…"

"Why is he after you, like *you* in particular?"

"Most likely because I hunted him, and because he knows I'll kill him if I get even half a chance."

Helen suppressed a shiver at the ice in Luciana's words.

She's a killer, no wonder you're attracted to her, psycho.

"I'm not doing a very good job of cheering you up," Helen apologized. "I have a whole folder of memes for this, but that's not very helpful, seeing as you don't have a smartphone."

"What's a meme," Luciana raised her eyebrows. "And what makes a phone 'smart,' exactly?"

"Ok, well, bear in mind that I don't have the vocabulary to explain most of this, but memes are basically an art-based language made popular on the internet," she explained. "They're a kind of cultural short-hand for conversations used by the younger generations."

"The internet?"

"Oh jeez," Helen let out a long, slow breath. "Alright, so it's like this…"

They spent the next few hours covering pop culture, trends, and major historical events that had occurred since Luciana sequestered herself away. By the time the sun was setting, they were closing in on the Kansas-Colorado border.

"So where in Colorado are we going, exactly?"

"A wolf sanctuary," Luciana announced.

"A wolf sanctuary?"

"Yes," Luciana closed the book and tucked it down beside herself. "Rescue Wolf, I think it's called. A friend started it in the sixties. I'm not sure if it's open to the public, now that you bring it up, but I know that was his plan back when it started."

"Damn," Helen tried not to show her excitement. "That's really cool."

"It's a great mission," Luciana nodded. "Wolves have been unfairly hunted, almost to extinction—just like the Fae were once upon a time."

"The Fae were hunted?"

Helen glanced over and saw a melancholy frown on Luciana's face.

"Yes. Fae existed before modern man, at least we think we did. We were born of your faith and imagination, your first beliefs and your most primal fears. For a while things were fine but…well, let's just say witch hunts didn't just kill free-thinking human women."

"I'm sor–"

She froze mid sentence as she turned back to the road and her train of thought was instantly derailed. A man, or a man-shaped creature, was running alongside the car through the trees and grass. It was massive. Easily ten, maybe twelve feet tall with elongated arms and a hunched, gorilla-like posture, but it easily kept pace with them at seventy miles per hour.

"What the hell?" she turned back to Luciana, who was staring at her in puzzled worry.

"What's wrong?"

"There's a…" Helen turned back, only to find the creature was gone without a trace.

If it was ever there in the first place, nutjob.

"S-sorry," she shook her head, doubt pouring into her mind like a bucket of chilled poison. "I thought I saw something, uh, but I think I'm just tired."

"Oh, shoot," Luciana looked out the window with surprise. "No wonder you're tired, you've been driving for hours. Let's pull off somewhere and grab some food?"

"Sure, we could get some fast food."

"Ugh," Luciana stuck her tongue out. "I was hoping that was just going to be a fad."

Helen laughed hard enough for her belly to hurt.

"Fast food? Not a chance," she managed at last. "Fast food is *everywhere*."

"Great," Luciana frowned.

"Well, we could find a sit-down place?"

"Actually, I may have a better idea," the woman perked up. "Last time I was out and about, they were just putting in these 'rest areas,' safety stop areas on the highway that–"

"You'll be happy to know that those are still around," Helen winked.

"Why don't you pull off the next time you find one of those," Luciana smiled sweetly. "I'm sure I can whip something up!"

"Alright," Helen beamed. "Are you gonna use magic?"

"Yes," Luciana's laugh was infectious as she gave Helen a conspiratorial wink. "I think maybe we can get away with something small, don't you?"

Twenty minutes later the two women were pulling into a rest stop just across the Colorado border.

Aside from a pair of semi trucks, they were the only occupants of the large, gently sloped parking lot surrounding a drab, single-story building and a run down wooden playground. A half dozen streetlights shed patchy light on the asphalt, and provided just enough illumination for Helen and Luciana to see in their spot at the far edge of the space.

"If it was light out, you could almost see the mountains if you looked over there," Luciana nodded as she stepped out of the vehicle and stretched widely.

Helen admired the woman's curves as her back arched like a cat and tightened her shirt against her chest.

"You don't mind if we sit on the hood, do you?"

"Nope," Helen got out and hopped up on the hood of the car, her eyes caught between the dark silhouette of the woodline and the murky sky.

"Great!"

Luciana climbed atop the hood as well, and scooted over close to Helen, closing the distance until their hips touched and their hands intertwined.

"Wine?"

"Yes, please," Helen's voice was breathy as she struggled to contain her growing desire.

"My pleasure," Luciana smiled. "Hold your hand out."

Helen obliged, holding her hand out with her fingers slightly spread, and impressed herself by not flinching as a wide, full glass of white wine appeared, the stem between her fingers and the bowl in her palm.

"That's never going to get old."

Luciana laughed as an identical glass appeared in her own hand and took a sip.

"Could we maybe have some snacks?"

"Of course," Luciana snapped her fingers lightly and a small wicker basket appeared in her lap.

The basket held sliced cheeses, bread, grapes, strawberries, and summer sausage—all perfectly ripe and delicious looking.

Helen's mouth watered at the sight, and she snaked out a hand and picked up one of the strawberries. It was firm, brilliant red, and—as she quickly discovered—sweet, juicy, and lush.

"Oh my god," she mumbled through a mouthful of berry. "This is literally the best fruit I've ever eaten!"

The pair ate amidst warm conversation, their wine glasses refilling at an interval short enough to explain their laughter growing louder, and the night chill disappearing.

"I wish we could see the stars," Helen sighed some time later, her head resting gently on Luciana's firm, muscular shoulder, and her wine glass held loosely by her side.

"I could do something about that," Luciana turned her head and kissed the top of Helen's head.

"Wouldn't that be too big of a deal?" Helen sat up straighter. "Couldn't it attract attention?"

"Sometimes little things make a bigger impact than you'd think," the woman smiled.

Luciana closed her eyes, a tiny furrow appearing between her eyebrows. A moment later, six loud pops broke the silence of the parking lot and Helen jumped in surprise as all of the streetlights crackled and went out, plunging the area into total darkness.

Helen blinked rapidly as her eyes adjusted to the thin light of the crescent moon. The moonlight was soft and weak, but Helen gasped as a river of white stars appeared overhead. Millions of pinpricks of light filled the sky in perhaps the clearest view Helen had ever seen.

So that's why they call it the Milky Way.

"Oh Luciana, it's amazing!"

"I wish you could have seen it a few centuries ago," Luciana smiled wistfully. "Before electricity, before cities were so…*big*."

"It must be hard," Helen nodded. "Watching things change so much. Watching the world move while you just…um…"

"Stagnate?"

"I was going to say something else," she frowned. "Something kinder."

"Immortality is a blessing and a curse. I have formed so many friendships with mortals over my many lifetimes, and every one of them has ended the same way: I watch them wither and die, then their children, then their grandchildren, and on and on, until even my memory is a ghost."

Chapter Two

Helen woke gently—a rare treat—and stretched widely, or at least as widely as she could. Her hands and feet hit the doors of the sedan as she rolled on to her back in the backseat. She blinked blearily, fumbling for her glasses and finding them on the floor of the car.

"Luciana?"

She yawned, sitting up, pushing her hair back out of her face, and looking around.

She took in the sight of the empty wine glasses in the passenger seat, her bra draped across the headrest of the seat, and her pants, socks, and shoes rolled up as an impromptu pillow.

It was chilly, even in the car, so she crossed her arms over her chest and peered out through the fogged up windows. She could see the outside world only as blurry shapes and shades, so she pressed her palm against the glass and smeared away the condensation.

Luciana was outside, sitting cross legged on the ground a few feet away from the vehicle, with her face turned up to the morning sun and her eyes closed.

Helen smiled, then quietly opened the door and looked around. After confirming that they were the only occupants of the space, she gingerly set her bare foot on the asphalt beside the car. It was cold and damp, rough and raw on the tender sole of her foot. She took a few steps to cross the sidewalk towards Luciana then froze as she was discovered.

"Have a seat," Luciana smiled, her eyes still closed. "If you'd like."

Helen looked at the grass, all sparkling with morning dew and lush looking. But also very cold and wet looking.

"Um," Helen looked around herself.

With no dry land in sight, Helen decided to press her luck while keeping herself dry. She straddled Luciana and sat gently in her lap wrapping her legs and arms around the woman and resting her chin on her shoulder.

Luciana was warm and enveloping, like sand on a sunny day at the beach. When the woman's arms wrapped around Helen's waist, she sucked in a breath of surprise that turned into a comfortable sigh.

"Hope this is ok?"

"Always," Luciana cuddled closer. "Are you aware you aren't wearing any pants?"

"I'm wearing boyshorts," Helen laughed brightly, wiggling a little on Luciana's lap. "Plus, there's no one else here."

Luciana's hands settled on Helen's waist, her fingers lightly but firmly holding her in place as the heat between them grew.

"Not worried someone will pull in?"

"Nah."

They clung together for a time—it could've been an hour or it could've been a lifetime, Helen didn't care so long as it didn't end any time soon.

Eventually though, it had to.

"We should get going," Luciana breathed into Helen's ear.

"Noo," Helen whined, squeezing her tighter.

"Come along," Luciana rolled her eyes with playful emphasis, standing up while easily lifting Helen. "I'd like to get to Arlen's in the daytime. He can be very cranky at night."

Luciana carried her with ease back to the car before setting her down gently. Helen tugged her pants back on with a minimum of complaining and, pulling her backpack from the backseat, retrieved a few items. With another glance around, she pulled her shirt off, balled it up, and tossed it into the backseat.

She stole a look at her passenger as she grabbed a replacement and was pleased to see the woman's eyes sparkling and a smile on her face.

"Like what you see?"

"Very much so, thanks," Luciana laughed.

Smiling, she put her hair up in a messy bun and pulled on a new shirt before getting out a toothbrush and a bottle of water. She rummaged around for toothpaste and her hand hovered over the pill bottles still rattling around the bottom of her bag. Her hand shook as she considered, but she pushed her doubts aside and left the pills where they lay. A moment later, she found her toothpaste and settled back into the seat.

"Arlen," Helen rolled the name around on her tongue as she started to brush her teeth. "Arlen, what kind of name is that anyway?"

"Irish," Luciana answered, looking as put together and refreshed as always.

"Mmm," Helen spit, then rinsed out her mouth before shutting her door and putting on her seatbelt. "Where did y'all meet?"

"Oh, it's a long story," Luciana smiled wryly. "I think it was the…fourteen hundreds? France and England were at war, and Agincourt had just gone badly for the French. I was moving around a lot back then—I was quite young—and I found myself suddenly behind the English lines–"

"Luciana, how old are you?"

"We didn't really keep track of the years back then to the same degree as you do now," Luciana apologized. "But the best I can figure is that I was born around thirteen hundred, maybe thirteen ten."

Helen let out a low whistle, eliciting a small frown from Luciana.

"Is that alright?"

"Yeah, no," Helen smiled apologetically. "It's just a lot to take in, you know? Like, there's a certain magnitude to that."

"Blech," Luciana made a face. "I have *magnitude*?"

"I didn't mean it like that, honest. I'm just so…"

"Young?"

"Well, that too, yes, but I was going to say 'temporary' or maybe even 'insignificant.'"

"You're *not* insignificant, Helen," Luciana answered with a sudden fierceness. "You're not, ok?"

Helen was quiet. Obviously, she'd known that Luciana was older—far older than any human could ever hope to live—but the idea of living with someone who had been around since the middle ages was…intense.

"Does my age make you uncomfortable, Helen?"

"Not uncomfortable, per se," Helen ventured. "Just a consideration, I suppose."

"It is important to me that you feel comfortable, that you don't feel manipulated, or–"

"I'm going into this with my eyes open, Luciana," Helen put a hand on the woman's thigh. "I'm not a dewy-eyed, eighteen year old."

"You're also not seven centuries old," Luciana countered. "Fae have a reputation for being manipulative, and it *is* well-deserved. Many of my siblings wouldn't think twice about twisting their words to get what they wanted from a mortal without a single thought for their welfare."

"Do *you* intend to deceive *me*? To manipulate me?"

"I already did deceive you, rather resoundingly, remember?"

"Fair," Helen frowned. "Do you intend to do that again? To betray my trust or hurt me?"

"No," Luciana's single word was as hard as iron.

"Well, then we take it slow until we figure out what this is. What we are."

"So you still want an 'us?'"

"Yes," Helen smiled and leaned over to give Luciana a peck on the cheek. "Very much so."

"Alright, but–"

"But the conversation isn't over," Helen nodded, surmising her intent as she fired the engine up. "No it's not, but it's *started*, and that counts for a lot, Ok?"

"Ok."

"Now," she said, putting the vehicle in drive and heading back to the interstate. "Tell me more about Arlen?"

"Well, when I was very young–"

"Meaning like twenty, or meaning two hundred?"

"Closer to the end of my first century," Luciana smiled. "Fae usually reach physical and intellectual maturity between sixty and one hundred, give or take."

"Not emotional maturity," Helen prodded.

"Who says we ever get that?" Luciana laughed.

"Ok fair," Helen rolled her eyes.

"I was around one hundred," Luciana continued. "I was living in Azincourt, having moved up from what's now called Morocco, where I was born."

She's Moroccan?

"Arlen was older than me," Luciana's gaze was distant, a faint smile on her lips as she looked out the window. "He must've been about…oh, three hundred? Maybe four?"

Helen stifled her jealousy.

"We Fae were more visible back then, people still believed in—and respected—us. He fought like a demon, had a reputation all throughout the British Isles and Scandinavia, and he was lending his sword to the English at the time."

"Were you a soldier too?"

"Me? No, not back then," Luciana shook her head softly. "I was traipsing my way through the world, making easy money at taverns by tricking over-eager idiots out of their coin, and I bumped into this...wildman. I saw him drinking a bunch of English soldiers under the table and thought I'd found some easy marks. I didn't realize he was Fae, at first; it's sort of something you develop as you get older and more powerful, so he, erm, took me by surprise."

Luciana looked over and seemed to notice the redness of Helen's face, her expression faltering.

"S-sorry, Helen."

"It's ok," Helen lied through her teeth, jealousy coiling inside her like a venomous snake. "It was hundreds of years ago."

"Really? Cuz it seems like it's bothering you."

"It is," Helen blurted out. "But I'm trying to be chill about it because otherwise I'm being totally psycho."

"Helen," Luciana reached a hand out and set it gently on her thigh. "It was a long time ago, there's nothing but friendship between us now. We *had* a romantic relationship, if you want to call it that, but it wasn't what a human would call serious. It was more like…"

"Like?"

"Like a fling," Luciana winced. "We were only together for a decade or so before things evolved into friendship. He's the one who inspired me to be a dragon hunter, actually."

"So we're going to visit your hunky Viking warrior ex, who is also a dragonhunter," Helen grumbled past reddened cheeks. "What could possibly go wrong?"

"So…subject change then?"

Helen couldn't keep herself from smiling at the desperate grin on Luciana's face as she broke the silence of the past twenty minutes.

"Sorry, yeah."

"There is no debt," Luciana nudged her gently, pulling another smile out of her reluctant lips. "What else do you want to know? Anything at all."

"Ok," Helen chewed her bottom lip a moment before an idea came to mind. "Ok, you said your powers were diminished now that you'd left home, what did you mean?"

"Ah, now that is a good question," Luciana nodded. "Fae are like…well, they are like rocks on a trampoline. We create little indents where magic can pool around us, so to speak. The longer we stay in one place, the deeper the pool and the more magic collects there. What's more, the magic *attunes* to us. It's easy for us to use, and hard for any visitor to utilize. That's why many Fae live in one place after they finally settle."

"After they settle?"

"All Fae go through a phase of wanderlust, then, we almost all find a place to settle down and grow."

"So, how long had you been at Casa de Rosas?"

"I moved there in 1836, shortly after I lost Askarii."

"Will you tell me what happened?"

"Helen–"

"Not *now*," Helen interrupted quickly. "Just someday, maybe."

"I'll try."

"Ok, so then–"

"Oh, turn here," Luciana pointed.

"Um," Helen rolled to a stop on the empty highway, looking at the open cattle fence towards which Luciana was pointing. "*There*?"

Luciana nodded, smiling, so Helen turned back to look at the rugged dirt road the woman had indicated. The path wound out into the rolling hills and broken, craggy ground and then quickly fell out of sight.

"Isn't this someone's property? Aren't we going to be trespassing?"

"Do you trust me?"

After a moment, Helen decided she did.

She turned her small car off the asphalt and rumbled cautiously onto the rocks and dried dust of the path, ignoring the sound of gravel pinging off the underside of the vehicle.

They meandered through the diciest driving of Helen's life for the next forty five minutes. They hugged the corners of roads that bordered steep cliffs, muscled their way up steep inclines, and coasted down roads she wasn't sure she'd be able to drive back out of, until they finally rounded a bend and found themselves on a smooth, gently sloping area of land that seemed to cover a few square miles. She could see hundreds of yards of chain link fencing that appeared to divide the property into large, perhaps even multi-acre enclosures. Off to the side, there was a round, two-story building with solar panels on top and a half dozen teepees, all clustered around a number of small out buildings and a greenhouse.

Helen squinted and was able to pick out several people walking around in a variety of workwear, all tramping about the place and elbow deep in different chores. After a moment, she could tell that their vehicle had been noticed, as a few folks paused in their duties to look in her direction, including a slim, blonde figure who immediately headed toward the main building.

"There's a lot of people here…"

"I see that," Luciana seemed surprised. "Don't assume anyone knows *anything*, ok?"

"Got it–"

"But, erm, don't assume they don't. You know?"

Great.

Two minutes later, they were pulling into a flat, dusty space beside the main building, and a group of four workers had paused long enough to congregate nearby.

"Here we go," Luciana smiled, opening her door and stepping out.

"Yeah," Helen breathed. "Here we go."

Helen followed the woman out of the car and found herself hanging timidly beside her.

"Howdy y'all," one of the workers waved. "Name's Liam, what can I do ya for?"

"I'm actually looking for–"

Luciana paused, then her face brightened.

"Arlen!"

Helen followed her gaze and caught sight of a mountain of a man who was coming around the side of the building. He was an easy six-and-a-half feet tall and every bit of two hundred and fifty pounds. He had long, shoulder length blonde hair, and rippling, chiseled muscles. He wore a pair of worn denim jeans and work boots, but no shirt to hide his turtle-shell abs or bulging arms.

He was also *covered* in tattoos in dark blues and blacks.

"Holy shit," Helen found herself drinking in the sight of the man and felt an extremely unexpected heat flushing her chest and tightening her stomach.

"Careful," Luciana said, wrapping an arm around her waist and whispering into her ear. "You'll make *me* jealous."

"Amanar," Arlen burst through the group of workers and wrapped Luciana in a massive hug, lifting her and spinning her around. "God, I haven't seen you in *ages*!"

Amanar?

"Let me down, you brute," Luciana laughed, playfully smacking the man on the shoulder. "And let me introduce you to–"

"Hopefully to this beautiful flower," Arlen's voice dropped a note as he casually set Luciana down with one arm and used his free hand to take Helen's and bring it to his lips gently. "Please, another minute without your name could break my heart."

Helen—despite her best efforts—swooned.

Something about the man's brilliant blue eyes, the timbre of his voice, and the wide, pearly smile he was flashing, was conspiring to fog her mind and raise her temperature.

"This is Helena," Luciana glanced down and made meaningful eye contact. "And I'm going by Luciana these days."

"I see," Arlen raised an eyebrow. "You new-age hunters always change your names so often. Come on, follow me."

Arlen turned, showing his broad back to them and forging ahead.

Helen turned to Luciana and mouthed *'Helena'* as unobtrusively as she could.

Luciana nodded and Helen was suddenly brought back to her encounter with The Smiling Man.

There's power in a name.

Helen followed quickly, as her hand was still captured by Arlen's, and she took a moment to study the scene depicted in ink upon his back. A pack of wolves all ran in circles around a full moon, which was centered between his shoulder blades. It was intricate enough that Helen felt like, if she just waited long enough, she'd see the animals start to move.

"Where're we going?" she asked after a few minutes of brisk walking, unable to see much past the man's broad shoulders.

"Luciana didn't tell you," he said, surprised. "I thought you'd like to see my work, my family."

"F-family?"

Her question was followed by a long, low, mournful howl. First one, then a second, and then a dozen more notes joined the first in a symphony of hair rising beauty.

"Here we are," the man propelled her forward.

Helen stumbled over a rock and nearly fell to her knees, but caught herself against the metal fence that appeared in front of her. She gripped the cold steel, ignoring the sting of her impact as she found herself face-to-face with a long white snout and profoundly deep, yellow-brown eyes.

She froze as a deep, primitive piece of her brain was reduced to its most simple instincts. Fight. Flee. *Freeze*. Her brain screeched to a halt, even as her eyes took in the massive, fluffy white canine in front of her. It was big, much bigger than she'd imagined, and it was standing stock still at the edge of the fence, apparently just as entranced as she was.

"H-hi," Helen squeaked, then flinched as the creature's tongue reached out and flicked through the fence to run a warm trail across the bridge of her nose.

"This is Magpie," Arlen beamed, the spell of silence broken. "She's the matriarch of this particular pack."

Magpie huffed and Helen fell backwards onto her butt unceremoniously.

"Har har," Helen glared at the now laughing Arlen.

"Here, let me help you," Luciana's tone had a bit of an edge to it as she offered a hand to Helen and helped her to her feet. "Be a little gentler, Arlen."

The man raised his hands in defense, but did not apologize, instead he continued his explanation.

"Magpie, or Maggie as we usually call her, came to the mission about twelve years ago," Arlen's ever present smile turned sad. "She's coming to the end soon, but until she does, she'll lead this lot."

Arlen gestured and Helen found herself finally realizing another dozen pairs of wild eyes were looking out at her from the brush and trees behind Magpie.

"Wow," now that her fear had subsided, Helen found herself enthralled with the wolves. "They're beautiful. How many live here?"

"In this pack? Fourteen."

"This pack, meaning more than one?"

"Yes, we have five packs at a time, give or take. We always take the dynamics of the group members into account, and of course it changes based on how many rescues come in."

"Arlen," Luciana interrupted. "This is great but we should talk."

"Come now, Luciana," Arlen seemed miffed. "You haven't seen me in two centuries, surely you want to catch up."

Helen felt a tingle of electricity in the air as the two locked eyes, but finally it was Luciana who broke first.

"Of course, Arlen," she sighed. "I meant no offense, please continue."

Helen noted the unspoken conversation taking place, but was not privy to the particulars. She felt like a child standing between grown-ups, unclear of the meaning of the tension, but certain that she was involved.

"I think your home is lovely," Helen broached a new direction in the conversation, subtly reaching out for Luciana's hand and intertwining their fingers. "And I would love to see more of it."

Arlen escorted them around the property, showing off each of the enclosures, and letting Helen get an up-close look at each of the five families of wolves. Magpie's pack was twice as large as any of the others, but all of the packs seemed happy and thriving—even the little trio at the far end of the space.

"So what exactly do you *do* here?" Helen asked as they passed a greenhouse on their way back to the main building.

"I live here, with a small group of volunteers who help me tend to the wolves and do the mundane bullshit that I don't want to handle; grant applications and stuff."

Somehow, Helen found it impossible to picture this man at a computer filling out an application for funding.

"And your volunteers, are they…"

"Human?" he guessed. "Yes, they are."

Helen tried to decide how to delicately ask her next question.

"No, they don't know," he continued. "And it'll stay that way."

"So why this?" she asked instead. "Why rescue wolves?"

"We Fae have a soft spot for broken things, and I am no exception."

Helen stumbled but kept her pace, ignoring a look from Luciana and turning her gaze inward.

Broken things like me?

Chapter Three

"So, what's with the teepees?"

Helen shivered slightly, despite the roaring fire a few feet in front of her. She was sitting next to Luciana—along with most of the workers at the sanctuary—around a broad bonfire that was putting up a valiant fight against the darkening sky.

"Oh," Mel, a young, brawny runaway who had apparently been here for several years, took the liberty of answering her. "It's kind of a *thing* around here. Basically, anyone can come out and volunteer at the sanctuary, right?"

"Ok?"

"Well, your first year, you're on your own," she explained, sipping mulled wine from a cracked mug. "You can stay here, but you have to handle your own lodging, food, all that shit."

"So…"

"So after a year, we all get together and build you a teepee!"

"Wow, that's pretty wild," Helen took a closer look at the teepees surrounding them. "So you made all these?"

Each was a unique structure—different sizes, different colors, a wide range of decorations, and homey details that made them so much more than just shelter.

"That one's me," Mel continued, pointing out a bright, robin's egg blue teepee covered in painted flowers. "Home sweet home."

"Yeah and after two years, you get to participate in the communal food fund," this time it was Derek, a gangly thirty year old who spoke up. "That's the real perk."

"Speaking of food, where the heck is Arlen?" Liam looked over his shoulder.

"I'm here, I'm here," Arlen's voice preceded him into the clearing. "Hold on."

He appeared a moment later wearing a loose, unbuttoned red flannel, and his jeans and boots from before. In one hand, he was holding a large metal pot that was billowing steam and had a ladle sticking out of the top of it. In his other, he had a basket stacked with wooden bowls and a stack of spoons.

"Chili," Liam perked up. "Fuck yeah."

"Never seen someone get that worked up over chili," Helen snorted into her mug of wine.

"You haven't had this man's elk chili before," the man countered, grabbing a bowl and spoon, and helping himself to some of the piping hot food. "It's legendary."

"Elk?"

"Yeah, elk," Liam laughed. "You ain't got any of them down in Tennessee, do ya?"

Helen didn't respond, distracted instead by Arlen drawing close to her and offering the basket of dishes.

"Eat up little one, the nights are cold here."

"She'll be fine," Luciana almost growled, eliciting a wry grin from the man.

Helen grabbed a bowl and spoon, and ladled a bowl full of the thick brown chili. It was brimming with chunks of onion, meat, and at least three types of beans.

And it smelled amazing.

Garlic, oregano, cumin, and a dozen other spices wafted up from the dish and Helen was salivating in no time.

"Luciana?"

"Thanks," Luciana took only a very small portion before indicating he should move to the next person.

Odd.

The talk turned to deeper topics as the daylight waned and the night truly fell. Helen was content to listen to some of the more exciting stories—the close calls, the rescues, wildfires, and blizzards—and eat in silence, and Luciana seemed happy to do the same. The roaring fire died low, and though it still put off a surprising amount of heat, Helen found herself cuddling closer and closer to Luciana's heater-like body.

One by one, the crew all headed off to bed until only Arlen remained.

"Ready to talk," his tone was serious now, a distinct turnaround from his jovial interactions with the workers. "Or shall we sit a while more?"

"Yes," Luciana said, leaning forward eagerly. "I have questions, and there are precious few I trust from the old days."

"Word travels fast," he nodded. "When Casa de Rosas disappeared, I admit, I feared the worst."

"No, he hasn't gotten me yet," Luciana set her jaw. "Only now I have…considerations."

Helen noted the quick flick of Luciana's eyes in her direction.

"I see that. It's been a long time for you–"

"That's not something I want to talk about," she cut in. "Please."

"What *do* you want to know, then?"

"Is Tetiana…"

"She is, last I heard."

"Who is Tetiana?" Helen piped in, determined not to be completely ignored.

"She's my sister," Luciana sighed. "The one I told you about.

She turned her focus back to Arlen.

"Do you know where she is?"

"Last I heard, she was in San Francisco," Arlen scratched at his chin. "Doing well for herself, as far as I know. She was in…oh what do humans say these days, 'entertainment.'"

Luciana quirked an eyebrow and Helen was glad she wasn't the only one left confused.

"She was never one to lay low, Luciana, you know that."

"Right, San Francisco."

"San Francisco is a big place," Helen pointed out. "Can you be a little more specific?"

"That depends," Arlen smiled and Helen noted that his teeth were much pointier than they had been before. "I owe Luciana favors, but *you*? I don't owe you anything."

Helen gulped, then looked down at the empty bowl beside herself.

Do I owe him now?

"Don't worry," he chuckled darkly. "Food and shelter are free of debt, when they are the product of politeness and custom."

"She will remain without debt to you, Arlen," Luciana scowled. "So *I'll* ask the question. Can you be more specific?"

"Careful, even your credit is not unlimited," he seemed nonplussed. "But ask around for an Armory, somewhere near the Castro District, I think. Follow the breadcrumbs and I'm sure you'll find her."

Helen felt a shift in the energy, a sharpness to the air, and a tingling at the base of her neck, not unlike what she'd felt meeting Magpie. She couldn't place exactly *what* had changed, but there was a growing sense of danger in the air and it was emanating from their host.

"The Smiling Man visited me a few days ago," Luciana changed the subject. "Do you know if he's been seen since?"

"No, he's been laying low since the forties. I take it he still holds a grudge?"

"It seems that way, yes."

"Then you'll be wanting to stay here tonight," Arlen licked his lips. "Shelter from The Smiling Man is a costly favor. I would be risking much."

"And you'll have my gratitude–"

"I'll need more than gratitude," he dismissed her. "You know what I want."

"You've changed."

"Like you did, all those years ago? You went into hiding for two centuries while the rest of us dealt with the fallout."

Chill filled the air between them and Helen shivered from more than cold.

"Fine," Luciana stood up abruptly, all but snarling.

She flung her hand out toward Arlen and a five foot long spear appeared, burying its silver head in the ground at Arlen's feet after shooting across the clearing.

"The last person to wield this was–"

"Yes, it was Askari," Helen could see water welling up in Luciana's eyes. "You know its history as well as I do, or nearly so."

"I do."

"Then you know how much it hurts to part with it," Luciana took a step forward. "Rest assured, it will be mine again."

"Have a good night, Luciana," the man stood and tugged the weapon free before turning his back on them. "Helena."

Luciana was seething and Helen was nervous to touch her, but she fought the urge to cower and instead, stood and wrapped her in an embrace from behind.

"Hey."

"Sorry, Helen," Luciana sighed, her shoulders dropping in defeat. "Maybe it was a mistake coming here."

"We got the information you needed," Helen gently turned her around. "Right?"

"At what cost?"

Helen didn't know what to say, so she kept quiet.

"Come on," Luciana nodded. "We should get back to the car before Arlen starts his hunt."

Hunt?

The trip back to the car was quick and quiet, with nothing but the whistling night winds and the semi-silent padding of heavy, furred feet in the enclosures beside them.

They passed the teepees, some of which had lights on inside, and they passed the handful of vehicles parked in the area, before finally reaching Helen's car.

"This isn't going to be very comfortable," Helen sighed. "Is it?"

"Oh, I don't know about that," Luciana smiled. "Here we have the protection of Arlen's magic, so I could probably make a few changes."

Helen smiled, trying and failing to conceal her excitement.

"Watch this," Luciana whispered conspiratorially.

Helen stared as the woman closed her eyes and held her hands out toward the small sedan they'd arrived in. She could hear *something*, like rhythmic music just soft enough to make her question its existence. Moonlight and shadow played tricks on Helen's eyes, masking the first changes of the vehicle, but within a few moments the transformation was too drastic to ignore.

The vehicle stretched and shuddered, glass sparkling as it changed shape and molded to a new, much larger frame. The front of the car elongated, as did the rear, until the metal and glass finally settled into the familiar and nostalgic shape of a classic station wagon.

"A shaggin' wagon," Helen laughed. "Very hip."

"Hey, I'll have you know these were *groovy* back in the day."

Helen's eyes sparkled with mischief as she ran a hand along the cool metal of the car. The roof was one long window, and she could see that most of the back of the vehicle was taken up by a mattress.

"Alright, I've gotta admit," Helen pulled open the passenger side door. "This is pretty sweet."

She didn't catch Luciana's expression but she could hear her smile as she climbed into the cab and stretched herself out on the bed. It was divine. Soft, plush, and ever so slightly cool to the touch. If she closed her eyes, she'd have no idea that she wasn't in some posh hotel.

"Comfy?"

She smiled without opening her eyes, able to feel the heat from Luciana's whispered words.

"Mhmm."

Luciana settled in beside her, her body hugging Helen's curves, and a hand coming to rest gently on her stomach, just below her navel.

"Luciana," Helen opened her eyes, losing herself immediately in the woman's gaze. "What did you mean 'Arlen's hunt,' earlier?"

Luciana's face turned slightly sour, her head propped up by one hand and backlit by the moon above.

"Arlen has always been very…feral," she explained. "In all the centuries I have known him, he has been a hunter, a warrior, a killer. I doubt the elk you had for dinner was hunted in a way you would call conventional. He is a shifter, and among other things, he prefers the bodies of beasts—prefers to feel blood on his claws and teeth when he satisfies his hunger."

Helen shivered, partly from fear, true, but also from excitement. The way that Luciana spoke, the passion that laced her words as she casually discussed transforming into a beast and hunting—killing—wild animals was…invigorating.

You're sick, you know that?

"And have you ever…?" Helen gulped, breathless. "*Hunted* like that?"

"Why?" Luciana leaned in close, her breath hot on Helen's neck and her lips barely touching her earlobe. "Are you hoping I'll say yes?"

Helen felt goosebumps break out along her entire body.

"Your heart is beating more rapidly," Luciana continued, her voice a sultry whisper. "I can feel your temperature rising and *smell* your fear?"

What is wrong with me?

"So you have," Helen managed past a gulp.

"I have."

Teeth nipped at Helen's earlobe, but they were sharply pointed—not the smooth flat teeth of a human being.

"We all have to satisfy our hunger, don't we?"

Helen gasped against her will and pulled back in shock. Luciana's lips were parted in a hungry smile, and Helen could see her teeth had grown more pointed—most especially her incisors and the corresponding teeth on her bottom jaw, all four of which were longer now and dagger-sharp.

Luciana's eyes were blazing, her pupils slightly elongated, and the color changed to dusky gray, her lips were full and red as ever, drawing Helen in.

"Too much?" Luciana's eyebrow raised and she pulled back, pre-empting Helen's kiss.

"No," Helen said, too quickly to excuse.

Her cheeks flushed and she felt the growing heat in her body.

"No," she considered how to ask what was on her mind. "But maybe, erm, maybe we could *pretend* that I thought it was and…um, well you could, er."

"Do it anyway?" Luciana smirked as Helen stumbled over her words.

Helen nodded, unsure what Luciana's smile meant for her.

"Well," Luciana traced a hand down Helen's body, her fingernails lengthening and sharpening as she did so. "Do you have a–"

"Zebra," Helen blurted out, as much to keep herself from moaning as anything else. "Let's do zebra."

"A prey animal," Luciana's hand worked its way back up to the side of Helen's face, where she could see her nails—now claws—glinting in the moonlight overhead. "How appropriate."

Luciana's voice turned to a growl on her last words and Helen found herself genuinely afraid.

"Come to think of it, I am rather hungry," Luciana sat up beside her and Helen could see her ears had lengthened and had little tufts of black hair at the tips.

"I–"

Helen's words turned to a strangled moan as Luciana raked a hand down her body, her nails leaving bright red scratches on her skin and easily shredding her thin shirt.

Her skin tingled and burned from the pain and the sudden coolness of the air, and her shirt clung limply to her sides as she bucked against Luciana's hand. She moved instinctively to sit up but the larger woman pressed a palm down on her chest and shoved her back against the mattress with enough strength to knock the wind out of her.

Helen squirmed under the pressure, which was just enough to let her breathe while reminding her she was helpless.

Luciana leaned down as if to kiss Helen's lips, but turned aside at the last moment and pressed her lips against her throat instead, sending another jolt of fear down her nerves. The stronger woman removed her hand from Helen's chest just long enough to grab both of her wrists and yank them up over her head, where she held them clamped together in one strong hand. The pressure was enough to hurt, but that only served to stoke Helen's fires further.

Helen arched her back once more as Luciana's hand slowly worked down her arm to her throat. It lingered there a moment, her powerful fingers wrapping firmly around her throat and tightening to the point where her jaw opened involuntarily, and she felt a rush of blood in her face. She choked out a gasp as Luciana released her and continued her journey down Helen's body. Her claws left more red streaks as she pulled them along Helen's collarbone and down to her breast, which she tortuously circled before drawing her claws up and around her nipple.

The woman's tongue and lips were driving her mad as they danced along the pulsing vein in Helen's neck, and the pain and pleasure mixed until she could no longer tell which was which. Her jeans were a formality at this point, she was soaked with anticipation, but she was trapped by both Luciana's muscles and her pacing.

"Please," she managed at last as Luciana drew her hand across Helen's stomach and down to her hip, which rose to meet her.

"Beg."

The single word, accompanied by a deep, powerful growl that vibrated Helen's entire chest, was enough to send Helen's whole body into tremors.

"P-please, Luciana, I want more. I need more."

Strong hands gripped her jeans and she-

Hands? Then how is she holding your wrists?

Helen glanced upward to see a pair of spectral, glowing red copies of Luciana's hands holding her wrists tight.

That raises some interesting possibilities-

She squeaked as Luciana jerked down on her jeans, pulling them down to mid thigh, and pulling Helen's arms taught at the same time. Warmth and pressure pressed against Helen's inner thighs courtesy of Luciana's tongue, distracting her as her pants were pulled the rest of the way off.

Helen's legs sprang open the instant her pants cleared her ankles, revealing her underwear and the growing dampness in the center of them. Helen's eyes closed in anticipation but…nothing?

She squirmed, pushing her head upward to glimpse down her body. Luciana was sitting up on her knees, her eyes glowing menacingly in the darkness, and her breaths heavy.

"Luciana?"

The tension mounted as Luciana leaned slowly forward, her hands pressing down on Helen's thighs and rendering her immobile. Another growl, lower and more guttural than before, rumbled past Luciana's lips just as a beam of moonlight struck her face. Her jaws, slightly elongated and brimming with sharp teeth, were parted a half inch or so, and her eyes were merciless orbs of hunger.

"L-L-Luciana?"

Luciana's tongue snuck past her teeth, running swiftly across her lips and wetting them slightly, and Helen's eyes widened in shock. Luciana's human tongue had been replaced by something much longer, thicker, and sporting thick ridges.

Helen opened her mouth to speak, but her voice rose into a shout as Luciana lunged forward, burying her face in between Helen's legs. Sharp teeth tore away the fabric of her underwear and a wave of sharp points and firm, strong strokes of her tongue had Helen speaking gibberish almost instantly. The appendage was far more flexible than any human tongue—it was damn near prehensile—and it roved up and down her labia, skirting past her clitoris and diving across her vulva from top to bottom and back again.

Helen's legs bucked, and she fought hard against Luciana's iron grip but strain as she might, she couldn't move an inch.

The tongue lashing was almost too much, it had her shivering and jerking within moments and just when she thought it might cross the threshold, she cried out again, this time as she finally felt Luciana's tongue penetrate her. It moved and writhed within her, filling her almost to the point of pain but stopping short. She drew a ragged breath, trying to make her body adjust to this new and tantalizing intrusion, but Luciana was relentless.

In and out, harder and harder, the tongue withdrew and slammed back into her. Helen would swear it was growing slightly with every pulse, but she was beyond herself. The ridges stroked past her g-spot on the backstroke, and brushed against her clitoris on the forestroke, a steady rhythm of pleasure that threatened to drown her.

When her climax finally came, it came like a tsunami. She bit her lip hard enough to bleed but couldn't stop herself from crying out—heedless of the noise she was making. Luciana was not gentle, and she did not relent, instead she continued thrusting, twisting, and nipping at Helen's sex until she was sweating, breathless, and quaking.

"Z-zee," Helen whispered between convulsions, her eyes crossed and her head light. "ZeEebra."

Lucian withdrew immediately, and just as quickly the hands pinning Helen down disappeared.

Helen blinked and, as her eyes swam into focus, she saw that Luciana had returned to her normal form, her former clothing hanging in tatters from her reduced frame.

"Are you ok?"

Helen couldn't speak, but she reached up with both arms and pulled Luciana to her, their chests and lips meeting and their legs intertwining.

"That was fucking amazing."

Chapter Four

"You could stay a while, you know," Arlen handed Luciana a steaming mug of coffee. "I was…impolite yesterday."

Helen barely held back a scoff.

"Seeing you again unexpectedly," he glanced over at Helen and seemed to judge her silently for a moment. "It brought up an abundance of feelings."

"I was an unannounced guest," Luciana smiled, dipping her chin slightly.

"There is no debt," the pair spoke in unison.

"Thank you," Helen blurted out. "For letting us stay here in your home."

"You dance close to the fire, young one," his eyes gleamed. "Take great caution that you do not burn up."

Spooky.

"I'll take care of her," Luciana wrapped an arm around Helen's shoulder protectively.

"I'm sure you will," Arlen's smile was sadder than Helen expected. "But you should know a few things before you leave."

Helen could feel Luciana's muscles stiffen.

"Such as?"

"Tetiana was still restless, young at heart when you last saw her. She has likely changed a great deal," his eyes flicked to Helen's and then back again. "And old foes still linger, perhaps darker and more dangerous than before."

"Menacing," Helen observed dryly. "Cryptic, but menacing."

Arlen burst out in a loud, raucous belly laugh that easily reached his eyes.

"She's a firecracker, Luciana."

"You have no idea," Luciana rolled her eyes at a beaming Helen.

"She means, I'm a handful in the sack," Helen flashed a peevish smile.

Really, marking your territory? Insecurity much?

"Well, that would make both of you," he replied just as innocently. "Though I can only vouch for one, of course."

Ouch.

Luciana cleared her throat uncomfortably and caught Helen's eye.

"I suppose that explains why she was willing to transform into a–"

Helen's sentence cut off with a squeak as her mouth shut of its own accord. She tried to open it, to offer some kind of retort, but her lips were sealed as though they'd been superglued. A moment of panic was followed quickly by a deadly glare in Luciana's direction. The taller woman was blushing deeply, despite her tan complexion.

"Well," Luciana cleared her throat again. "We'd best be off."

Luciana opened her arms for a hug and Arlen nearly lifted her off the ground in return.

Helen desperately wanted to make a snide remark, but she was still silenced.

"And you, human," Arlen took a step toward her and bowed low, then kissed her hand like she were royalty. "Keep that spirit of yours, and look after this one."

She was somewhat mollified by his response, but she kept up the appearance of being sour until after they'd climbed into the car.

"Sorry," Luciana was chewing her lip and looking sheepish as Helen neared the highway once again.

"Can I?" Helen tested her mouth and found that she could once again speak. "That was *rude*."

"I said I was sorry–"

"Why did you do that," Helen interrupted. "You didn't have to do that."

"Helen, you must not reveal what I can do to other Fae," Luciana frowned. "It is *dangerous*."

"Even to an 'old friend' like Arlen?"

"Even to him," Luciana answered grimly. "But I am sorry for doing that to you."

"What if I don't forgive you?" Helen lifted her chin high.

"Then there would be a debt," Luciana frowned.

Ooooh!

"That's a slightly worrisome smile," Luciana pointed out, her eyebrows raising.

"Maybe I like you owing me a debt."

"Helen, don't."

Helen was surprised at the hurt in Luciana's tone. She looked over and saw the crestfallen expression on the woman's face and it was almost enough to make her pull over.

"Hey, hey," she reached over and set a hand on Luciana's thigh. "I was mostly joking…what's wrong?"

"Debts are not optional for Fae," Luciana struggled. "They are…*compulsory*. I don't want to owe you anything for the same reason I don't want you to owe me anything. I like what we have. I like that it is mutual and real and I…I don't want it ruined."

"Luciana, listen to me," Helen tried to make her tone as serious and somber as possible. "There is no debt, ok? You don't owe me anything."

"Then I'm forgiven?"

"Not yet," Helen shook her head. "I'm still a little ticked about that."

Luciana opened her mouth to object but Helen held a hand up.

"There's no debt, you don't owe me anything, and in time I'll get over it."

Helen rolled to a stop at the point where they would be turning back onto the blacktop road. She looked left, then right, and was turning back to the left when she froze. She flicked her eyes back to a stand of aspen about one hundred feet away. The thin trunks were swaying lightly in the breeze with nothing untoward about them.

But for just a moment, she'd seen it again. Whatever *it* was.

"Luciana?"

"Hmm?"

"I think I saw something."

"What?" Luciana sat up straighter and looked around.

"It was like an animal of some kind," Helen's voice shook. "It was big, and fast, and–"

"Ah," Luciana relaxed a little. "It was probably Arlen following us to the edge of his territory."

"Ah," Helen gulped before turning out onto the road. "Right."

"How long is this drive supposed to take?" Luciana sighed heavily from the passenger seat a few hours later.

"Twenty-one hours, not counting stops."

"Ugh," Luciana rolled her neck. "How do humans *do* this?"

"Well, we don't exactly have a choice," Helen retorted.

"How many hours have we been on the road so far?"

"This is getting dangerously close to 'are we there yet' territory."

"Sorry."

"Six hours," Helen yawned widely. "We're six hours in and I'm starving."

"Can we pull off somewhere?"

"You read my mind."

It wasn't long before a billboard caught their eye. It featured a blown up picture of a sizzling pot roast, complete with carrots and potatoes, and a tall glass of iced tea.

"Jo-Ellen's," Helen snorted. "Sounds like a roadhouse."

"What do you know about roadhouses?" Luciana laughed. "Come on, anything sounds better than being in the car right now."

"Your wish is my command," Helen shrugged, flicking on her blinker and pulling off onto the exit.

Five minutes later they were pulling on to the crushed gravel that served as a parking lot for the restaurant, which looked like it had been built in several stages over the years. The core seemed to consist of a repurposed trailer home—possibly with an attached shed—but various chunks had been added on essentially one room at a time.

"Huh," Luciana smiled. "Well, it's definitely unique?"

Helen didn't answer, but she, too, was intrigued by the warren of mismatched walls and roofs.

There was only one other car in the lot, a black '67 impala in mint condition.

"Now *that* is a thing of beauty," Luciana remarked as she stood and stretched for a moment in the sunlight.

"You think it's the owner's? Seems like a badass car for someone who runs a diner."

Luciana just shrugged and waited for Helen to lead the way.

Or it could belong to The Smiling Man, and he's waiting to kill you inside.

Helen's footsteps faltered at the thought, but she didn't want to embarrass herself in front of Luciana.

If she thinks I can't handle this, she'll ditch me in a heartbeat.

The door, clearly labeled with a bright red and white welcome sign, swung open with the jingling of bells. The room revealed was warm, wooden, and filled with all kinds of knick-knacks and Americana. One wall was covered in hubcaps of every shape and size, the top of the walls was rimmed with license plates from across the country, and various cast iron pans, old farm implements, and other tools were hung up all over. There were a few tables, all covered in red and white checkered plastic tablecloths, but most of the seating was in the form of booths along the inside and outside walls.

"Sit anywhere you like," a rough male voice called out. "Be with ya in a second!"

"Booth?"

Luciana nodded and Helen selected a booth near the corner. She was about to sit down when Luciana stopped her, a sheepish look on her face.

"What?"

"Can I, uh, can I take that side?" she glanced at the entrance to the restaurant. "I don't like to sit with my back to a door."

"Sure," Helen shrugged, moving around the table.

"Thanks."

Am I crazy, or did she just let out a sigh of relief?

Well, you are crazy, so.

She was saved from further introspection by a giant of a man emerging from a door on the far end of the room. He was tall and gangly like a giraffe, with shoulder-length dirty-blonde hair and a goofy, lanky gait. He had a dirty apron on over a pair of 90's jeans and a flannel shirt, and he wore rugged hiking boots.

"Hi, uh, Sean," Helen read the man's name off of a small plastic badge on his chest.

"Hi," he smiled briefly but warmly before pushing his hair out of his eyes. "Welcome to Jo-Ellen's, what can I get ya?"

"Er," Helen looked at the empty table. "We still need menus."

"Shit, right," Sean pulled a pair of folded paper menus out of his back pocket and set them on the table. "Sorry, most of our customers are regulars who've been coming here for years."

"Got it," Helen laughed, skimming the menu.

"So are you Jo, or Ellen?" Luciana smiled brightly, laughing loudly with her eyes.

"Oh, hah, yeah no it's named for some old friends, actually."

"Sean," another, much rougher voice shouted from beyond the doorway. "Quit flirting with the hunters and tell me what to cook damnit!"

"Ok, uh we have *new* customers, Dan," Sean stammered back. "So maybe chill a sec!"

"Pretty casual atmosphere here."

"What did he mean by hunters?" Luciana scowled.

"Hunting is pretty big around here," Sean's response was a bit clipped and distant. "Most folks that come through here are hunters. Why, you're not vegetarian are ya?"

"Hardly," Luciana smiled.

What is that about?

"Drinks?"

"Water for me, Helen?"

"Coffee, black," Helen smiled. "Small water, no ice please."

"You got it, I'll give y'all a sec," Sean turned to go, then stopped himself. "Almost forgot."

He set two napkin-wrapped sets of utensils down on the table in between them and then walked away.

Helen unwrapped the heavy silver utensils and set the napkin on her lap. When she looked up, she was surprised to see a look of absolute disgust on Luciana's face.

"What? What's wrong?"

"The flatware," Luciana frowned.

Helen looked down and saw that Luciana had opened her napkin but had apparently let the silverware drop.

"Are they dirty?"

"They're *silver*."

"Ok…?"

"Many Fae are…well, essentially allergic to silver," Luciana scooted the flatware aside with her napkin. "To some of us it just feels like microfiber, others have a more severe reaction. If *I* touched it by accident—without proper preparation—it would burn my skin and hurt like hell."

"Oh, shit so you mean these are *real* silver?"

"Yes, which presents another potential problem."

"What's that?"

"Ah, thank you," Luciana said loudly, indicating Sean's return.

He set their drinks down and pulled out a notepad expectantly.

"I'll have the pot roast," Luciana slid the menu back to him. "Carrots and potatoes please."

"Sure thing, and you?"

"Uh, pig 'n a poke please."

"Good choice, Dan's favorite. Anything else guys?"

"We're good, thanks."

Helen waited until the man had left the room again before turning back to Luciana.

"So? What the fuck?"

"I think these might be hunters," Luciana muttered, holding her hands flat together, palm-to-palm.

Helen squeaked in surprise as a quick flash of blue light covered Luciana's hands, and she instinctively turned to see if anyone had noticed, but they were still alone.

"What was *that?*" she hissed.

"I need to be able to touch the silver, otherwise they're going to suspect us."

"Luciana, what the hell are you talking about?"

"*Hunters*, Helen," she pointed at herself. "As in hunters of *Fae*."

"No, you really–"

"Solid silver utensils at a roadside diner?" Luciana frowned. "Seriously? Plus the water in our cups and your coffee is holy water."

"Holy water?"

"Yeah, it does fuck all to nintey-nine percent of Fae, but most of us think it stinks like hell," Luciana shrugged. "It has been popular since the middle ages, despite being totally pointless."

Helen felt her heart rate rising.

"Ok, hang on, joking aside…we're good right, we're safe?"

"No."

"What do you mean no?" Helen's mouth went dry.

"Hunters kill first and ask questions never," Luciana explained calmly. "It has always been this way. Usually it's younger Fae, and those who get attracted to big, flashy, often violent forms, who attract their attention, but they'll kill any of us they find."

"What do we do?"

"We blend."

A vein twitched above Luciana's eye, revealing to Helen that her partner was just as anxious as she was.

Not a good sign.

"But if it comes down to it," Helen glanced at the doorway. "You could, y'know, take 'em right?"

"It's hard to say," Luciana sipped her water. "They're tricky, dangerous, and resourceful. We have no way of knowing what they know or what they have back there."

"So—"

"So eat quickly, and let's get the hell out of here."

They weren't waiting long before Sean reappeared, this time accompanied by a slightly shorter, slightly broader man who Helen assumed must be Dan.

"We don't get a lot of new customers," Dan smiled in a way that raised alarm bells in Helen's mind.

"Told ya," Sean laughed. "Here you go."

The two plates of food were slid in front of the women, but the men stayed standing by the table.

"Thanks," Helen smiled, faltering a bit when neither man appeared to be leaving.

She forced herself to pick up her utensils, cut a small bite off of her meal and pop it into her mouth—which she did, miraculously, without trembling.

"Good?"

"Oh yeah," Helen said through the mouthful of food. "Amazing!"

It wasn't a lie either. The food was outstanding, but it was overshadowed by the thinly veiled tension in the room.

"Everything ok with the pot roast?"

Helen watched as Dan's hand settled casually on the handle of a large knife hanging at his belt.

Luciana smiled calmly, then reached out and picked up her fork looking for all the world like she had nothing to fear. Helen's breath caught in her throat as the woman's skin touched the metal, but nothing happened. She pulled off a bite of steaming brown meat and popped it into her mouth with a smile, chewing slowly and closing her eyes in obvious enjoyment.

The second she did so, Helen saw Dan's shoulders relax and his hand move from his knife.

"Truly amazing," Luciana said after swallowing.

“Well, you let us know if you need anything else, alright?”

They ate quickly and in silence, and by the time Sean returned, they were long past having cleared their plates.

“Room for pie?” he asked brightly. “We’ve got like, twelve kinds of pie.”

“Oh, none for me thanks,” Luciana smiled wide. “But that was all delicious!”

“Same for me,” Helen lied. “I’m stuffed.”

“Can we get our check, please?”

Sean seemed surprised at Luciana’s question, and for a moment looked unsure of what to do.

“Oh, shit, right,” he laughed and scratched the back of his head. “You know what, it’s on the house.”

“No, I insist,” Luciana’s eye twitched minutely. “We’d like to pay our way.”

“Honestly, we never even have customers this early in the day so–"

“Sean, you and Dan are great,” Helen interrupted, watching a faint tinge of pink rise in Luciana’s cheeks. “I’ll tell you what, I’ll make ya a deal!”

"Oh?"

"We'll take your free meal if you let us tip you, alright?"

"Sure," he chuckled.

"Great," Helen plucked a twenty from her purse and slapped it down on the table.

"That's too much."

"Too late," Helen laughed, grabbing Luciana's hand and pulling her out of the booth. "See ya around, Sean!"

They crossed to the door, opened it, and made a beeline for their car. Helen could feel Luciana's tight grip on her hand, but for all that anyone could tell she seemed as cool as ever. Helen didn't let go until they reached the car. She opened Luciana's door and headed to the driver's side. Helen could tell by her knuckles that Luciana was still worried and it took all her control not to peel out of the gravel lot on their way out.

"That was close," Luciana breathed shakily. "You could've gotten hurt."

"We're ok," Helen reached over and brushed an errant strand of hair back behind Luciana's ear. "We're safe."

"I should've picked up on that," Luciana shook her head. "I've lost my touch, I'm out of the loop. Since when do *hunters* run a damn *diner*?"

"Well I mean, what should they run? A grocery store?"

"A bar," Luciana was exasperated and her voice was rising. "Or a damn…*gun range* or something!"

Silence.

"Sorry," Luciana leaned against the window, her eyes closed.

"Luciana, how much trouble are we in?"

"I don't want you to worry, Helen."

"I *need* to worry," Helen pressed. "That much is obvious. But I'm flying blind here, I need to know what is out there."

Several minutes passed before Luciana finally answered.

"What do you want to know?"

"What are hunters, aside from the obvious?"

"Hunters have existed for a long time, probably forever," Luciana explained. "They've been killing Fae as long as there have been things that go bump in the night."

"So like, Van Helsing type shit?"

"Yes, anything supernatural though, not just vampires."

"Why though?"

"Because some Fae are dangerous, or cruel, or uncontrolled," Luciana shrugged. "Most of us adapted to the changing times, so you don't see it as much, but back in the day Fae were wilder, more dangerous."

"How were they more dangerous, that doesn't make sense?"

"Well, *guns* are pretty new in the grand scheme of things," Luciana frowned. "And a stake to the heart is fine and dandy, but you don't need one if you have a wood chipper."

"Yikes."

"Yea," Luciana pressed. "So essentially, the disparity between what the Fae could do to humans and what humans could do to us…Well in many ways the gap keeps closing. That doesn't stop people being terrified of all the monsters of their nightmares and stories, and it certainly won't help us if some hunter clocks me."

"Fuck," Helen blew out long slow breath. "So we have to worry about hunters, and The Smiling Man, and…what? What else?"

"The Smiling Man has a great deal of influence in certain circles," Luciana skirted the issue. "Or at least he did. I can't see that having changed in the last two centuries."

"So he has like, henchmen?"

"Something like that, yes," Luciana nodded. "I should've…I should've planned for this, I'm so sorry, Helen."

"There is no debt," Helen patted Luciana on the thigh and turned her focus back to the road. "We'll figure it out."

Will we?

We have to.

Unless you're in a pretty padded room talking to yourself, putting yourself into some buddy-cop horror drama television show. No wonder you don't want your medication—you'd have to go back to reality.

Shut up.

Chapter Five

"You sure you're still good to drive?" Luciana asked some time later.

The sun had dropped below the horizon, taking with it the light of day and revealing a clear, purple-and-black sky overhead.

"I'm alright," Helen blinked a few times to wet her dry eyes.

Was I staring again?

"Not too tired?"

"Nah," Helen lied.

Movement blurred at the edges of Helen's vision, dragging her eyes away from the road. Whatever had been chasing them-

Nothing.

Whatever had been chasing them before was still following, if it was even real. Now there were two of them, in fact, if her eyes were to be believed. The shadowy figures loped along either side of the darkened highway, always staying out of the beams of their headlights and always matching their pace—despite the fact that Helen was going almost eighty.

If that had been all, Helen might not have had a white-knuckle grip on the steering wheel or sweat at the base of her spine.

Helen's eyes darted around, flitting from shadow to shadow both inside the car and out in the world. The edges of the darkness were undefined, they shifted slowly but surely when she was focused elsewhere. Some grew, others shrank, some formed tantalizingly familiar shapes, and others flickered at the edges of her vision.

Helen took a breath and focused her mind on pushing them back, on forcing them back into the docile, static things she *knew* were real.

But it wasn't working.

"Helen, you're making me a touch nervous."

She glanced over at Luciana's face and found it marred by darkness. Her beautiful eyes were ringed by hollow shadows and her mouth—currently turned down in a frown—flickered between a toothy, too-wide smile, and her pursed, plump red lips.

"Helen?"

"I'm fine," Helen could hear the quake in her own voice, but she held it together enough to smile softly at Luciana before turning back to the road.

"Helen, pull over."

"Really, it's–"

"Now."

Helen felt a layer of unyielding steel beneath Luciana's soft voice and pulled off to the side of the road before flicking on the car's hazard lights.

"What's going on?"

"I just need some air," Helen managed past a tightening chest. "One second."

She popped the door open and caught herself on her seatbelt in her haste to get out. She angrily clicked the button and stumbled out into the quiet darkness of…wherever they were.

Sand and gravel crunched beneath her sneakers as she walked across the headlights and stepped off the side of the road. She could feel her heart pounding like it was going to break through her ribcage and her head was light with panic. She took great gulping breaths to no avail, and she could feel her blood starved of oxygen no matter how much air she drew in.

A horse and flea and three blind mice

Sat on the corner shooting dice

The horse, he slipped and fell on the flea

Whoops, said the flea, there's a horse on me!

Boom, boom, ain't it great to be crazy…

"Shut up," Helen hissed. "Shut up, shut up, shut up!"

She kicked a rock off into the darkness, then recoiled at the rattle and hiss of a long black snake that slithered up beside her.

"Helen!"

Helen flinched, stepping back instinctively as the light from Luciana's door opening revealed not a snake but a dry, bent branch laying in the sandy soil beside the car.

"Fuck," Helen shivered despite the warm air.

"That's it," Luciana put her foot down—literally. "I'm driving, and we're pulling over in the next town."

"We've gotta get to–"

"Yeah, we've gotta get to San Francisco," Luciana propelled Helen gently back into the car, then shut the door.

Helen tried the door handle and found it wouldn't budge.

Trapped again, trapped again–

"Right," Luciana settled into the seat beside her. "Do you want to talk about it, do you want to sleep, or is there another way I can care?"

"Hah," Helen found herself suddenly fighting tears. "I *wish* I could sleep."

"I could help with that, you know."

Helen perked up.

"Really?"

"Yes. I could wake you up when we find a hotel, too."

"Please?"

Luciana looked over at her with a melancholy smile.

"Of course."

Helen woke with a start, sitting bolt upright and blinking in the daylight that was pouring into her tired eyes. She looked around, confused for a moment by her surroundings. She was laying in the bed of the station wagon, wearing a pink sleeveless t-shirt and a pair of darker boxers, and locks of her hair were plastered to the left side of her face by drool.

Her body was heavy, like her limbs were filled with sand, but she managed to throw off the thin blanket covering her and rub the sleep from her eyes.

Glasses?

She looked around blearily and found her glasses next to a bottle of water beside her pillow. She picked them up and flinched at a rattling sound that accompanied her movement.

Looking more closely—not to mention more clearly—she could see that her bag of medications was tucked in the blanket next to her water, along with a note.

Helen,

No pressure, I didn't know if you'd need these when you woke up. If you're reading this instead of talking to me, it means I'm probably sunning on the roof.

XO

-L

Helen ground her teeth and ignored the medications, opting instead to unscrew the cap on the bottle and take a swig. Rather than a small drink she found herself slamming the entire bottle—why was she so thirsty?

Time to face the music.

Helen scooted down the length of the vehicle and shoved open the back before stepping out into the outside.

They were out of the mountains now, though Helen didn't recognize her surroundings. Scrubland extended in every direction and the air was heavy with a surprising heat.

"Helen?"

She turned and saw Luciana sprawled out on the roof of the car, her head propped up by a pillow and her body covered by a slinky crimson bikini. The woman sat up, the faintest sheen of sweat on her gloriously tan body, and brushed her hair out of her eyes.

"How are you feeling?"

Helen pursed her lips and took stock a moment before answering.

"Ravenous," she stretched and felt her joints popping and creaking in protest. "Where are we? I feel like I slept for a year."

Maybe you did.

"Not a year," Luciana smiled apologetically. "About thirty-six hours."

"What!?"

"Helen, you needed rest."

"You were gonna wake me when we got to a hot–"

Helen stopped mid-syllable and glared.

"Let me guess," she crossed her arms. "We didn't go to a hotel, ergo you weren't technically lying?"

"Correct."

Luciana's kindness and caring were obvious, but her lack of apology still pushed Helen's buttons.

"I thought you were done deceiving me?"

"I'm not going to apologize, Helen," Luciana frowned. "I put you to sleep at *your* request, and your body did the rest."

"Oh," well that took some wind out of her sails. "You didn't keep me asleep?"

"No, I just waited for you to wake up naturally."

"Oh, um," Helen couldn't maintain eye contact, so she looked off into the shimmering haze of the distance. "Where are we now?"

"Western Nevada."

Luciana slid to the edge of the roof and then to the ground with a fluid, cat-like grace that hitched Helen's breath.

"About four hours from San Francisco, actually."

"You d-drove all night," Helen stuttered despite herself as the woman sauntered forward to within a few inches of her.

"Like I said, you needed rest," Luciana wrapped her arms around Helen's waist and pulled her close. "And I need *you* to be healthy and whole, ok?"

She "needs" me?

Yeah, right, I guess she can lie after all.

Shut up.

"Ok," she managed, pulling the taller woman close and laying her head against Luciana's chest.

Luciana smelled of summer—fresh air and wildflowers filled Helen's nostrils; the woman's skin was as warm as an old wooden beach chair, but as soft as a summer breeze.

"Hey."

Luciana's arms drew her tight, holding her firmly but comfortably against her larger frame.

"Are we going to talk about what's going on?"

"What do you mean?" Helen mumbled evasively.

"Helen, you're not taking your medication," Luciana's gaze was like a laser drilling through the back of Helen's head, but she tamped down the urge to look up. "And I'm a bit…worried."

"Can we *not* talk about it?" Helen gulped. "At least for now?"

Afraid to tell her she isn't real?

"Ok," Luciana gently kissed Helen on the forehead. "But I have conditions."

Helen risked a glance upward and was held captive by the concern filling Luciana's stormy eyes.

"Conditions?"

"You have to tell me if you get to a point where you feel unsafe," Luciana started, pulling a hand back and holding up a finger. "You have to promise me we're going to talk about *why* you're making the decision—when you feel comfortable doing so. Finally, if you do something to endanger yourself or that makes me believe you're going to get hurt, hurt yourself, or hurt someone else you need to understand I'm going to intervene."

"What does intervening look like?" Helen squeaked.

"Whatever it takes to keep you safe," Luciana's jaw set firmly as she waited for Helen's answer.

"Ok."

"Ok?"

"Ok, I agree to your conditions."

Helen felt a pull in her chest and opened her eyes in surprise. A shimmering green thread wove its way out of her shirt, then shot across the scant inches to Luciana's hand where it wound itself into a ring around her pinky finger, then disappeared in a shower of sparks.

"Whoa."

"Yeah, it's a little dramatic these days, I imagine," Luciana apologized. "But a few centuries ago that got a pretty good reaction from petitioners."

"Petitioners?"

"People who come to make deals with the Fae."

"So we've '*made a deal*?'"

"After a fashion, yes," Luciana smiled softly. "Except that, unlike most Fae deals, this one just lets me look out for you—even if you argue with me about it."

What did I just sign up for?

"Does it always look like that?"

"Yes, or at least every deal I've ever done looked like that."

She's done other deals…

Shut up.

"So I guess that's where the saying 'pinky promise' comes from?"

"You know," Luciana laughed. "I actually have *no* idea."

Helen sniffled loudly, her eyes watering despite their shared laughter.

"Hey," Luciana pulled back and lifted her chin with a soft, slender finger. "Why the tears?"

"You're not, um," Helen's cheeks were wet with tiny rivers of worry. "You're not th-thinking I'm too crazy? Or, or you wanna leave?"

"Oh my sweet Helen," Luciana crushed her in another—more possessive but still tender—embrace. "No, baby, I'm not going anywhere. Your 'crazy' doesn't scare me."

"It doesn't?"

Helen's question was delightfully muffled by her face being buried in Luciana's breasts.

"No," she answered softly, stroking Helen's hair. "I've got crazy of my own, love, I think we all do."

Love?

"Listen, I haven't been in a relationship in two hundred years," Luciana chuckled. "I'm bound to mess *something* up, but it won't be this. It won't be caring too little, or leaving when things get difficult."

Helen bit back a sob and felt her knees going weak. Life had taught her one thing with exceptional clarity: no one stayed. Once the curtains were drawn back and the extent of her damage was known, *no one* stayed.

She won't either.

"I'm not going anywhere," Luciana whispered, holding her firmly and keeping her on her feet. "Not as long as you'll have me."

Five hours later, they hit the edge of San Francisco.

Luciana was driving again, which didn't bother Helen at all. When she'd asked about it, Luciana had simply pointed out that she hadn't driven in fifty years and that she'd missed it.

Fair enough,

The suburbs were crowded, but the highway kept them out of the urban tangle for quite a while. When they hit the city proper, however, and slid over to an exit ramp, that changed pretty immediately. In a matter of moments, they were locked in a gridlock of cars and trucks. Helen glanced at the clock on the dash.

5:45.

"Fuck, what day is it?"

"It's Friday, why?"

"Rush hour," Helen rubbed her eyes in irritation."Evening rush hour. Everyone is trying to get home, traffic is going to be a mess.

Her prediction played out by the book. The din of a hundred idling engines, accompanied by the occasional beep of an angry horn, was like the droning of an angry mechanical beehive.

Of course, the cars themselves would've been bad enough if it weren't for the terrain. The city seemed to abhor flat surfaces and even streets, instead favoring an insane network of zigzags and the most unhinged hills that Helen had ever seen.

Even Luciana seemed a bit on edge.

Every corner they turned or light they passed through seemed to be accompanied by an incline that their poor car struggled to conquer, or else a dip that threatened to send them crashing into the people in front of them,

"What's with all these damn hills?" Helen was testing the strength of the door handle, squeezing it tightly as they dipped down almost vertical to descend another incline.

At least the hilly parts had *slightly* less traffic.

"San Francisco has always been hilly," Luciana answered, her tone clipped and her concentration obviously on the road. "It hasn't always been this fucking big though."

The car was heavy with anxiety, but after around an hour, they finally found themselves parked on the street in the Mission District.

"Where are we?"

"Dolores Park," Luciana took a moment to steady her breathing and crack her knuckles. "Sorry, I just need a second, that drive was intense."

"Totally," Helen agreed. "The roads here are on crack."

Luciana looked up sharply, meeting Helen's eyes with a questioning look.

"They're *what*?"

"On crack," Helen laughed. "It's, well it's probably problematic, but it's slang these days, just means 'crazy' or whatever."

"Ah," she relaxed and leaned back against her seat, closing her eyes.

Helen waited patiently, her hands in her lap and her mouth shut as her companion seemed to sink into meditation. A few moments passed without any input and Helen began to feel the walls of the car squeezing in on her, the air growing stifled. She needed to *do* something, not just sit here in silence. Finally, she couldn't take it any more.

"Where are we going?"

"Well, I actually don't know," Luciana made a face.

"You don't know," Helen repeated flatly.

"Correct, although I know Tetiana *is* here in the city."

"Luciana, there's like a million people here, please tell me you have *something* to go on?"

"I do," Luciana hesitated, piquing Helen's curiosity.

"And?"

"I told you that she's my sister, and that sisters are rare," Luciana fidgeted a bit. "Part of why we are rare is that we are *linked*. Being this close to her, it is only a matter of time before our magics draw us together."

Reassuring.

"Ok, so how does that work, exactly?"

"Well," Luciana's eyes widened and she pointed over Helen's shoulder. "Like that, generally."

Helen turned and saw…nothing. Just a normal city block with a by-the-slice pizza joint, a few small shops, the park itself, and an image painted on the side of a nearby building that depicted a buxom blonde wearing leather lingerie and holding a riding crop.

Helen's cheeks burned brightly and she found herself hoping her partner didn't notice.

Helen was *very* familiar with this particular woman.

She'd spent more than one evening enjoying herself while watching her videos online. She went by Styxx, and was easily one of the most famous pornstars in the world despite her…eclectic tastes. Helen knew she'd gone from star to producer to owner of a production company (though she still put out plenty of new content of herself to satisfy hungry fans like Helen), but she didn't realize she'd opened a *club*.

Still, the ad caught her attention, or maybe it was the scantily clad goddess and her piercing green eyes. Curling letters underneath the sign offered a simple but intriguing message:

"Psilo - Get Lost In The Magic"

Regardless, she thought as she filed the information away in her mind, there was no sign of a sister.

"Uh…"

"That's her," Luciana half-smiled, pointing at the billboard. "That's my sister."

Chapter Six

"Fuck me," Helen blurted out. "You're kidding."

"No," Luciana laughed. "Why? I take it she's famous since she's painted on a building."

"Yeah," Helen flushed crimson. "Uh, yeah she's famous for…um…well she's an adult entertainer."

"She's a stripper?"

"Um, more adult than that," Helen shook her head.

"Oh," Luciana was still laughing. "So she's a porn star, now why does that not surprise me– why are you blushing?"

"It's nothing," Helen laughed nervously. "Wh-what is our plan now?"

"Well, I guess we need to find out more about this 'Psilo' club."

"Good point, hang on," Helen pulled out her phone and tapped the screen, opening her internet browser and pulling up the club.

As soon as the page loaded, her phone's speakers erupted with loud sexual moans and deep rhythmic electronic dance music. She turned down the volume of her phone and refused to look over at Luciana's face for fear that she would lose it altogether.

"This page has next to no information," Helen scrolled further. "It looks like it's all password protected and there isn't even a place to register."

"Alright, maybe we should find a hotel in the meantime."

"Luciana, this place is super exclusive, I don't have any club wear, and I'm honestly not sure they'd let someone like me in anyway."

"Why not?"

"Well, I mean *look* at me–"

"Hey," Luciana reached out and grabbed hold of Helen's jaw, eliciting a sharp intake of breath as she was forced to face her. "Don't degrade yourself, especially not in front of me."

"Ok," Helen breathed. "S-sorry."

"And don't apologize to me, you should be apologizing to yourself."

Helen was caught like a mouse gazing up at a hungry housecat, utterly helpless in the woman's hand.

"You're gorgeous," Luciana continued. "Say it."

"You're–I-I mean, I'm gorgeous."

"Good girl," Luciana's steely voice was accompanied by a wry smile. "Now, use that phone to find us a hotel."

Helen gulped, nearly panting as Luciana released her and her insides turned to warm goo.

Holy shit

For once, all the voices in her mind agreed.

It took all of two minutes for Helen to pull up a map of the city overlaid with dozens of icons indicating hotel options.

"Well there's a shitload of options," Helen frowned. "But *damn* this place is expensive."

"Pick something nice," Luciana put her hair up in a short ponytail, a scrunchie appearing around her wrist out of thin air. "I want a big, comfortable bed, and a tub I can soak in. You know I don't care how much it costs."

Hot.

Helen selected the Bay Imperial—partly to be a brat and partly out of curiosity as to how the other half lived—despite the $1,300 per night price tag. The advertisement promised elegant, modern furnishings, and a couple's soaking tub in each room.

She punched in the address and the crisp, clear tones of her GPS crossed the car's radio.

"Turn left, then turn left."

Twenty minutes later, they were pulling up in front of a glass-and-steel monolith overlooking the bay.

"Gonna be hard to park this thing in the city."

"Did the world forget how to valet while I was away?" Luciana laughed, pointing out the window toward a sharply dressed man who seemed to be eyeing them from the doorway of the hotel.

"Right," Helen rolled her eyes. "I forgot I'm with a classy broad used to the finer things in life."

"Shut up and drive," Luciana winked.

The valet was a new, awkward experience for Helen but it was also, mercifully, fairly self explanatory. The bellhop looked surprised to see that the extent of their baggage was Helen's backpack and a rolling suitcase, but nonetheless moved as though to take the items from them.

"I'm fine," Helen shied away. "Thank you though."

They walked into the entryway—Helen like a shy teenager and Luciana like she owned the place—and up to a large walnut desk.

"Good afternoon ladies, how may I help you?"

"Reservation for Helen LeFitte?"

"Ah yes, the executive suite, here we are."

Luciana's eyebrows raised in a way that made Helen smile.

"And we'll need a card on file for the–"

Luciana reached into a small leather clutch she was holding and produced a black metal square the size and shape of a credit card. It had no name, no numbers, and no visible magnetic strip either.

"Oh," the woman's eyebrows nearly shot through the roof. "I-I…let me get my manager."

"What the fuck is that thing?" Helen hissed as the woman headed to the back.

"It's called a Praetorian Card," she shrugged. "It's a fairly…exclusive item. Armand told me a few decades back, that cards are the new method of legal tender these days."

"Yeah, a *credit card* is the new way to pay. That thing looks like you have to belong to some billionaires club to even–"

"Good evening ladies, I am Leon," a suave gentleman in a tailored armani suit not unlike Armand's appeared and gave a quick bow.

The man had a delightfully soft Italian accent that matched his perfect hair and immaculate charm. He was flanked on either side by women in similarly matching outfits, albeit with skirts instead of pants, and he oozed both professionalism and a polite, unobtrusive sort of 'at-your-service' air.

"May I?" the gentleman held out one hand toward Luciana.

She deposited the card in his outstretched hand and he held it up to the light, then flipped it over once, squinted at it, and finally handed it back to Luciana.

"Everything seems to be in order," he smiled widely. "It's been several years since we've had a praetorian member here, and on behalf of the Bay Imperial, I'm grateful for your organization's continued patronage."

Helen tried to maintain a polite smile, while Luciana looked for all the world as though this was the very service she'd expected.

"Brooke and Lily will be your personal concierge staff while you are staying with us, and will be able to attend to any needs you have whether here or at the hotel," he stepped up to the terminal at the desk. "It appears you booked the executive suite, but I can of course upgrade that to the presidential suite, if you would prefer."

"That will be fine, thank you."

"Very good ma'am," his fingers flew across the keyboard, letting out a staccato of sharp clicks before he turned his eyes to them once more and smiled. "Your room is ready now, if you require dinner service or *anything* else please don't hesitate to ask."

Leon pulled a leather folio from behind the desk and handed it to Luciana, who took it and shot Helen a sly wink.

"Your key is inside, and the elevators are just there, across the lobby. I truly hope you enjoy your stay."

Luciana led the way to the elevators, with Helen right beside her. While her partner exuded confidence and poise, Helen felt ungainly and awkward. Their 'concierges' were a few steps behind, their heels clicking softly on the tiled floor and reminding Helen of their presence.

"Luciana," she whispered as softly as she could, hoping her lover would hear. "I have no idea what I'm supposed to do. I'm out of my depth."

"Relax," Luciana whispered back, her hand snaking out and grabbing hold of Helen's.

The woman's warm skin and firm grip were like an anchor in the storm of Helen's social anxiety. She clung to it, squeezing perhaps too hard as they entered the elevator.

"We can wait for the next one–"

"Nonsense," Luciana interrupted Brooke with a wave of her hand. "Come on, hop in."

The two women stepped in after them. Brooke tapped a button at the top of the key panel, then scanned a badge against a small black box on the wall, then the women promptly pressed themselves against the sides of the elevator flanking the door. They both kept a neutral facial expression and stood as still as a pair of fashionable, modern statues. Brooke had dark brown skin and long, braided hair. She had the body of a track and field runner, with long lean legs and strong calves. Her nails were french-tipped and her frame was slight, despite being several inches taller than Helen. Lily on the other hand was about Helen's height, with thick, enviable curves, and shorter blonde hair that was buzzed along the sides and longer on top. Both of them were conventionally attractive, but they were so opposite each other that each accentuated the other even further.

Helen felt uncomfortably plain in her simple clothes and average build. She stared unobtrusively at Lily's wide hips and substantial bust, then over to Brooke's obvious strength and athletic proportions.

You're not even as pretty as the hotel staff. This city is going to eat you alive.

Helen scrunched her eyes shut to drown out the voice.

At least Luciana has options now, how long before you're discarded?

Helen's jaw clenched until pain shot up the sides of her head.

You can always call mommy.

She felt Luciana's hand squeeze hers and peeked through her shut eyes. Luciana was surreptitiously looking over at her as she applied firm, steady pressure to Helen's hand.

"Ma'am, are you alright?" Lily asked, causing Helen to look up and open her eyes in surprise.

"She has a hard time with elevators," Luciana interjected. "They tend to give her motion sickness."

"I'll have the hotel maintenance adjust the cables to make sure it's as smooth as possible," the woman produced a phone and tapped away furiously at the screen. "And if you'd like I can have dramamine brought up immediately?"

"Um," Helen shook her head softly. "Maybe just some ginger ale?"

"Yes ma'am," Lily nodded, firing off another message.

The elevator door dinged and slid open, revealing a wide, spacious sitting room.

"There's no hallway?"

"No ma'am," Lily answered Helen's question without a trace of judgment in her voice. "The Presidential Suite encompasses the entire thirty-third floor."

Luciana grabbed Helen's hand again and pulled her into the room while Helen simply gaped at the obvious wealth on display. The room was decorated with a plush couch, a large electric fireplace, a massive flatscreen television, as well as statues, art, and other tasteful touches.

"Wow," Helen spun slowly, her eyes settling on a wall of floor-to-ceiling windows. "This is *amazing*."

"Will you be needing anything? Dinner perhaps?"

Luciana turned at Lily's question, then looked to Helen.

"I'm not really hungry but maybe some wine?"

"Of course ma'am, we have an extensive cellar."

Helen waited awkwardly as the woman stared at her, her phone open and ready.

"We'll have something red, perhaps a Malbec," Luciana saved her again. "Preferably Argentine."

"Right away."

Lily tapped out another message on her phone and then looked back at the pair.

"Is there anything else we can arrange for you this evening?" Brooke spoke up at last. "Do you require tickets, reservations, or–"

"A-actually," Helen found her voice. "We need to get into a club, Psilo."

Brooke paused, her thumbs hovering over her touch screen.

"Psilo?"

"Tonight, and we'll need a car to take us there," Helen finished firmly.

"Yes ma'am…I'll make it happen."

Luciana pulled Helen close.

"That'll be all for now."

Whether Luciana's words were magic or simply the 'right thing to say' in this confusing, unfamiliar social setting, the two women nodded curtly and stepped back into the elevator.

Their absence left an odd quiet.

"So, this is how the other half lives," Helen grinned, feeling suddenly sheepish and awkward in the casual wealth displayed around the room. "This is how you're used to traveling?"

Helen moved toward one of the archways that separated the various sections of the penthouse, but Luciana held on tight to her hand.

"Oh–"

Helen barely had time to look back before Luciana gave her a sharp tug and she found herself pulled into the taller woman's arms.

"Hi," her cheeks burned and her voice was soft, timid.

"Hi," Luciana smiled back before leaning Helen back slightly and kissing her deeply.

A moan escaped Helen's lips and she clung to Luciana like a drowning sailor to a life preserver. Luciana's lips were full and soft and she tasted very faintly of dark red wine.

Then, just as quickly as it started, Luciana pulled back and left Helen hungry for more.

"Sometimes I would travel like this, yes," she let go of Helen's hand and ran a finger across the back of a chaise lounge as she walked about the room.

"When I was young, arrogant, and convinced of my own supremacy."

"Hmm," Helen's eyebrows rose and she followed along as Luciana led the way through an archway to what looked like a bedroom suite. "Castles and palaces I'd imagine, rather than high-rises."

"A few castles, a few palaces," Luciana winked. "A few princes, a few princesses."

Helen's cheeks reddened and she felt the familiar warmth growing inside of her as she imagined Luciana cavorting with gorgeous, wealthy royals. Her stomach twisted in knots as she warred back and forth between jealousy and desire.

"The beds are nicer now," Luciana nodded to a massive, California king with crisp ivory linens. "As are the castles."

Helen swallowed a lump in her throat as the woman climbed atop the bed, mussing the covers and presenting a clear view of her khaki-clad ass.

She's wiggling like that just for you.

Lucky us.

"Are you joining me, princess?"

Helen shut her mouth, noting it had gone dry, then scrambled to get out of her shoes and climb up beside Luciana, who was now laying on her back laughing with one knee bent and her hands out at her sides. The bed was soft, but not obnoxiously so. Helen's hands and knees sank a few inches into the plush mattress as she climbed up beside her partner, and in the space of a few heartbeats she was on her hands and knees beside the woman, looking down on her.

"Gods you're beautiful," Luciana murmured, reaching a hand up and cupping the side of Helen's face.

"I-I don't know about that," Helen felt the heat in her face grow to match the warmth of Luciana's skin.

"No no," Luciana's mouth curled up at the corner. "That wasn't a question."

Helen felt her knees tremble and was glad she was already on them—much less likely to hurt herself swooning like this.

"Come here," Luciana instructed her softly.

Helen obeyed and soon found herself cuddled beside the larger woman, her head on Luciana's arm and her body curled up along her side. It wasn't the raunchy, x-rated experience she'd been expecting, but in some ways it felt more intimate.

Or you don't measure up to the princes and princesses of the past.

"Helen, I want to talk about tonight," Luciana said finally, her fingers running up and down Helen's back and sending chills along her spine.

"Ok," Helen sensed hesitation in Luciana's voice. "What about it?"

"This club, 'Psilo,' is a Fae club," Luciana started, sounding nervous for the first time that Helen could remember. "We Fae tend to party erm…*hard.*"

Fun!

"Mhmm."

"You need to be careful," Luciana continued, now looking Helen directly in the eyes. "Everything will be alluring, everything will draw you in. The music will be better, the alcohol stronger, the people more beautiful."

"This doesn't sound so bad, what's the big deal?"

"The big deal is these places aren't meant to entertain mortals, they're meant to trap them."

Goosebumps raised on Helen's arms.

"Why are we going there then?"

"Because we have to find Tetiana," Luciana sighed. "If I could think of another way to do that without leaving you alone and in danger, we'd be doing that instead."

Helen chewed her bottom lip.

"Why is it so important that we find your sister, exactly?"

"Because of her lineage," Luciana paused, then continued softly. "She was an oracle, she was an oracle for *centuries*."

"Like, tell the future, magic eight ball, prophecies kind of oracle?"

"Yes."

"That's an *option*?"

"Not generally, no," Luciana seemed to grow agitated. "No one knows how oracles are made, or how to become one—not even oracles. She was 'chosen' to have the sight, and so, in the eyes of our people, she was off limits for the duration of her time as a seer."

"Wow."

What else was there to say?

Their wine—and Helen's ginger ale—arrived a few minutes later, delivered personally by Brooke. The woman seemed utterly unfazed at seeing the two of them in bed together. She uncorked the wine bottle, poured an inch or so into a crystal glass, then offered it to Luciana, who was the first to sit up.

Luciana swirled the wine, smelled it deeply, then took a tiny sip before nodding, indicating (apparently) that Brook could go ahead and fill their glasses.

Brooke did so with all the skill and ease of an experienced five-star waitress.

"I was able to secure you two tickets to Club Psilo, ma'am, and a driver will be here in an hour to pick you up," she turned to face Helen, who was still lounging. "Would you be needing any of our other club offerings?"

Something in the way she spoke raised Helen's eyebrows.

"Like?"

"Anything you might require."

“What do your clients usually request?”

“We have access to a wide variety of experience enhancement options for our clients who desire them,” Brooke was as stone-faced as a world poker player. “We find them particularly popular amongst the high-end club scene.”

“So you can get me an eight-ball?”

“Yes ma’am,” Brooke typed up and fired off a quick note. “Will that be all?”

“Holy shi–”

“She’s kidding, Brooke,” Luciana shot the flabbergasted Helen a look. “We won’t be needing that, but we’ll keep you apprised, thank you.”

“Very well ma’am,” Brooke was friendly but emotionless as she produced two bright silver and gold coins and placed them on the coffee table. “You’ll be needing these to enter Psilo.”

“Thank you, that’ll be all,” Luciana flashed another winning smile as their attendant departed.

Chapter Seven

"I wasn't gonna take it," Helen huffed quietly when the door to their suite closed a moment later.

Liar.

"We need to lay low," Luciana sidled up to her apologetically, her hands going to Helen's waist and their eyes locking. "Scoring cocaine is unlikely to help us do that."

"Neither is using the billionaire black card," Helen countered, though she allowed herself to be pulled close enough that she had to tilt her head up to look in Luciana's face.

"Fair enough," Luciana shrugged. "But since we're already here…"

"Mmm," Helen nodded. "Yeah, I guess it would be a shame to waste the reservation."

Helen stood on her tiptoes and planted a firm kiss on Luciana's lips, her arms draping across the taller woman's shoulders like a sixties bombshell. Luciana returned her kiss with passion, but she could feel her keeping her at bay.

"Easy now," Luciana managed to mumble around their deepening kiss. "We won't make it to the club."

Helen pulled back and pouted, her bottom lip sticking out dramatically.

"Besides," Luciana let go of her and sat on the edge of the bed. "I assumed you'd want to freshen up after so long in the car."

"Freshen up," Helen snorted, then froze in alarm. "Oh fuck, I don't have anything to wear to a *club*. I'm going to look like–"

"Helen–"

"–Some kind of vagrant," Helen started to pace, racking her brain as she sorted through her meager belongings in her mind. "Damnit Luciana, we should've gone to a store or somethi–"

"Helen!"

Helen stopped abruptly, caught off guard enough to break her spiral.

"I'm not going to let you go to a high-end club looking out of place," her tone softened—slightly. "Get a shower, I'll have something appropriate for you when you get out."

"Shouldn't *I* help pick out what I'm going to wear?"

"Do you have much experience going to ultra-exclusive clubs in major cities?"

Tell her.

Lie.

"Fine," she shot back. "Smartass."

Helen maintained eye contact as she pulled her shirt up over her head and tossed it carelessly on the floor. Next went her pants and underwear, again tossed haphazardly.

Luciana raised an eyebrow but said nothing, though her eyes drank in Helen's naked form hungrily.

"So can I get a prev–"

"Shower," Luciana interrupted firmly. "There'll be makeup for you if you want it, and an outfit out here."

Helen's thighs pressed together as her body responded to the authority in Luciana's voice, but she didn't give any indication of her growing heat. Instead, she spun about and sauntered off toward the bathroom.

An unexpected smack hit her ass hard enough to lift her left cheek and she let out a yelp of surprise before turning back in shock. Luciana was still across the room, but a wicked smirk played across her lips.

"Good girl."

Goosebumps popped up all over Helen's body and her eyebrows nearly shot through the roof. She could feel her face turning scarlet, so she turned and stepped out of sight into the bathroom. Before letting out the breath she was holding.

She did that on purpose.

She rolled her eyes at her ongoing, omnipresent internal conversation.

"No shit."

The bathroom was nice—though the large tiled shower was a bit of a letdown after Casa de Rosas.

Still, the room was spacious, tasteful, and bigger than any hotel bathroom she'd ever seen. There was a soaking tub big enough for two, or perhaps three if they were very comfortable with each other. A double-mirrored vanity, a wooden door labeled 'sauna,' and an open, large-but not-quite-walk-in closet rounded out the space.

Helen traipsed over to the shower and gave the knobs a spin. They turned easily and piping hot water gushed from a brightly polished square showerhead about the size of a dinner plate.

She turned her back to the shower, allowing bits of it to run in tiny rivers across her collarbones, between her breasts, down her stomach to her thighs.

You should get in and get out, you're on a timeline.

Helen obediently pulled some body wash from a fancy bottle on a small shelf in the corner of the shower and lathered herself up before rinsing off just as quickly and efficiently. The scents of exotic flowers filled the space as the perfumed soap mixed into the clouds of steam, but all that Helen could think about was the warm, earthy smell of Luciana.

Of course…you do have an hour.

Her inner monologue—aware as ever of her train of thought—goaded her not to indulge in the desires that filled her body. But despite the warmth of the water, the shower was no match for the heat between her legs. She replayed Luciana's low, sultry voice in her head a thousand times in the space of a second

Good girl.

She shivered against the heat and allowed one of her hands to slide down her stomach and rest between her legs. Her deft fingers spread out amongst the short, rough patch of prickles where her hair was growing back. She generally kept smooth—a personal preference—but somehow she didn't think Luciana was the type to mind.

The thought of Luciana had her raising her head and sliding her fingers lower, her middle and ring fingers gently parting her lips and drawing down the sides of her entrance. Her free hand roamed across her chest, kneading her breasts, teasing her nipples, and imagining that it was Luciana's firm, strong hands touching her.

Her lips parted in a soft moan as she dipped her fingers within herself, curling them to press up on her g-spot while applying a gentle pressure on her clit. She hadn't realized just *how* worked up she'd gotten until now, her own touch sent fire down her nerves and she felt herself backing against the wall to keep her feet. The relatively cool tile against her wet skin made her gasp. Her fingers worked inside, curling back and forth in a come-hither motion that fueled a burning pressure in her abs and chest. Her pace quickened and she applied more pressure through her palm to her clit, allowing the friction to increase with every thrust and curl of her fingers.

Her next moan was louder, and she clapped her free hand over her mouth to stifle the noise as her back bowed from the pressure of an impending climax.

Careful now, wouldn't want her to hear us, would we?

The idea that she might get caught had her hand tightening over her mouth—but despite her attempts to keep quiet, she hoped, *prayed* that Luciana would walk in and discover her. She would walk in, flash Helen that wry smile that she found so unbearably seductive, and join her in the water.

Perhaps her magic would play a role, or perhaps she would simply press Helen against the wall and finger-fuck her until she-

Helen's climax shook her body, buckling her knees for a moment while she whimpered with pleasure.

When the waves stopped rolling, she felt *better*, but not satisfied, not by a long shot.

"Damnit," she swore, her mind still playing through fantasies of the woman she'd run away with.

But the night was young, and after they talked to Tetiana she'd make sure she addressed her…*needs* more thoroughly.

The hot water made quick work of rinsing her clean again, and after running her fingers through her hair under the showerhead a few times, she turned the water off and stepped out. She left a trail of water droplets as she crossed the tile to the closet where a quick peek revealed stacks of fluffy, cream colored towels.

"Perfect," she wrapped one around her chest, and another around her hair.

A black bag was sitting on the vanity, inviting Helen's curiosity, and upon further examination, she found it was full of brand new luxury makeup. Lipstick, eyeliner, shadows, even brushes filled the bag. Unfortunately, Helen was more of a mascara-and-maybe-liner kind of girl.

She frowned, seeing the bag full of exotic products was more intimidating than inspiring.

"Almost ready?" Luciana called out from the bedroom.

"Yeah," Helen turned to the door in time to see Luciana appear there. She was wearing a black microdress with a series of cutouts down the front, each held together with a thin silver chain. The cutouts, which decreased in size as they neared her stomach, ended just below her navel and showed off her impressive musculature. The hips of the dress were ruched, with drawstrings pulling them upward into slits that rose to her hip bones and left precious little fabric hanging in front and back of her.

For footwear, she wore a pair of chunky black ankle boots, again adorned with silver fastenings.

Helen eyed the woman speechlessly, her gaze flowing up those toned legs, across her stomach to her barely held in bosom, up to the black choker around her neck and to the three sets of identical silver hoop earrings in her delicate ears.

"What?" Luciana cocked her head to the side as she ran a hand through her hair, tussling it perfectly.

"My god you're beautiful."

"Goddess," Luciana winked suggestively. "And so are you. Can I use part of the mirror?"

Helen nodded dumbly, allowing Luciana to step up beside her and lean in to get a better look at herself in the mirror.

She turned this way and that, frowning in concentration, then took a hand and passed it in front of her face. Helen blinked not in surprise but in awe as bold wings of eyeliner, heavy mascara, and dark lipstick appeared under her moving palm. Every bit of it applied perfectly, even the tiny insets of silver liner at the inner corners of her eyes.

"Can you do me?"

"You don't want to do your own makeup?"

"I'm not very good at it, is all," Helen shrugged in embarrassment. "Not like *that* anyhow."

"Of course I will," Luciana smiled warmly, her voice free of judgment. "*After* you get dressed."

Helen rolled her eyes, then headed back to the bedroom area of the suite. Her outfit was eye-catching, to say the least, and at least from the doorway, it looked like far too little fabric to amount to actual clothing.

Her first impression didn't change as she got closer and had a better look at the outfit laid out on the soft duvet.

A shimmery silver dress was laid out that, while more conservative than Luciana's, was still only going to go down to mid-thigh on Helen at most. She lifted the silky garment and noted it was backless, with nothing but a tie at the back of her neck and open space down to just above her hips. A pair of strappy silver heels, the kind that wind up around your calf, were set out next to them, as was a brand new silver purse on a chain. The final piece was a silver necklace with a black, heart-shaped crystal as a centerpiece. The gemstone sparkled, even in the relatively low light, and seemed to blaze from within.

No underwear?

She felt her face heat up

"So the coins, the jewelry, isn't that all a lot of silver," Helen raised an eyebrow. "I thought that was no good?"

"You don't like the color?"

"No it's not that, I just don't want to put you in any kind of danger, I mean–"

"Oh, it's all white gold," Luciana explained. "A favorite of mine that serves a dual purpose."

"Oh?"

"It throws off hunters," she winked.

That damn smile of hers.

"Luciana," Helen held the dress up doubtfully. "I don't really think I can pull this kind of thing off."

"You're hot, Helen," Luciana stepped up behind her, reached around and untied the towel covering her. "Own it."

Helen bit her lip, equal parts emboldened and aroused.

Do it.

She stepped into the dress, shimmying it up onto her hips and moving to tie it back. Luciana took the strands of fabric and worked them into an elegant bow for her, then reached down to grab the necklace. Helen held her towel-wrapped hair up as the woman set the stone around her neck and fastened the clasp, her heart in her throat and her breath held until Luciana's hands moved away.

"Now, turn around," Luciana instructed.

Helen did so and found her lover carefully studying her face.

"Alright, I've got it," Luciana waved a hand slowly in front of Helen's face and she could suddenly feel the presence of makeup on her face.

It wasn't heavily applied, and it didn't make her want to rub her eyes like it always did when she applied it herself, but she *could* feel it there.

"Can I…"

"Go look? Of course!"

Helen headed back to the bathroom and over to the mirror. Luciana had given her a silver shimmer on her lips, just enough to sparkle in the light while letting her natural color shine through, as well as fine, sharp winged black eyeliner over a thin streak of silver eyeshadow. She, too, had dark black mascara, but the tip of every eyelash was decked in bright silver—a feat she would've called impossible if not for Luciana's magic. Her hair had been styled too, with her loose flowing locks being replaced with valkyrie-style side braids and a gentle curl in the hair running down the top and back of her head.

She looked like a model, like someone out of an EDM fashion magazine.

"Luciana, I don't know what to say."

"You don't need to say anything," Luciana kissed her cheek. "Now get your shoes. I'm sure our ride is waiting on us."

Chapter Eight

The doors to the hotel lobby opened with a near-silent whoosh and Helen followed as Luciana stepped lightly out onto the tiled floor, her boots relatively quiet next to the click-clack of Helen's heels.

"Good evening, ladies," Brooke fell into step next to them, appearing as if by magic. "Lily has your car waiting outside, will you require accompaniment this evening?"

"No, thank you," Luciana smiled politely, her steps and attitude as confident as a runway model despite the jaw-dropped looks they were receiving in the lobby.

"Very well, ladies," Brooke fell out of step and nodded in deference. "We look forward to your return."

"I'm just going to say it," Helen blurted out as they stepped through the automatic doors from the atrium to the outside. "This shit is *crazy*. Who lives like this?"

"You can," Luciana turned to her with a serious face and a sparkle in her eye. "We can."

A moment later, they were standing under the wide canopy of the pull-through in front of the hotel. The air was cool, but not cold, and there was a slight breeze that smelled of saltwater and set the fabric above them rustling.

"I wonder what kind of wheels we got."

Helen's question was answered a few seconds later when a sleek, low-profile silver car with blacked out windows purred up to them. Lily stepped out of the vehicle and over to the pair of them, a tinge of red in her cheeks.

Is she embarrassed?

"I a-apologize for the wait," she handed over a leather and steel key fob. "The one-seventy-seven is stored specially due to–"

"Not a problem," Luciana stepped past. "Aston Martin, no?"

Aston Martin...like James Bond Aston Martin?

"Yes ma'am, one of only seventy-seven of this model ever produced" Lily stepped to the passenger door and pulled it open. "You are a fan of the brand, I hope?"

"Oh I've admired them for a very long time," Luciana trailed her hand along the hood as she stepped around to the driver's side.

She slid into the driver's seat just as Helen sat down on the passenger side of the small coupe. The interior was black leather, with a space-age instrument panel and an elegance that couldn't be over-stated. The navigational system inset into the dashboard had a pre-programmed destination—though the address had no name and appeared to be in an industrial area of the city.

"So this is the Bond Car."

"The what?"

"The Bond…the James Bond car?"

Luciana gave her a blank look.

"Nevermind," Helen struggled to explain. "We just have a lot of movies to watch, that's all."

"I've *loved* Aston Martin for a hundred years," Luciana traced the wheel. "You know, I once went to watch Lionel Martin race Aston Hill outside of Tring."

"I don't think I'll ever get used to this," Helen buckled herself in absentmindedly. "But I don't think I'll mind trying."

Luciana smiled in response and revved the engine, sending a pleasant vibration through the seat and a shiver up Helen's spine.

"Hold on tight."

When she put the car in drive and hit the gas, Helen could feel herself pushed back into the seat by the powerful engine. Her breath caught as they whipped out into the street and dove into the clogged streets of night-life San Francisco. The beast they were riding in seemed like a wolf among the sheep that were the other vehicles on the road, and Luciana wove in and out of traffic with a speed and precision that had Helen gripping her thighs.

Luciana might as well have been a formula one driver. She slipped through gaps that Helen would swear they couldn't fit through and then perfectly slide across multiple lanes.

"Jesus, were you a race driver or something?"

"I spent a summer bootlegging in 1922," Luciana mentioned offhandedly, as though that were a complete answer to Helen's question.

The further they got from the center of the city, the less traffic they had to fight. By the time they were nearing their destination, they were zipping through empty streets at a breakneck pace.

Helen glanced at the dash and could easily read the large digital readout—96 miles per hour.

"We should slow down, right?" Helen squeaked as they ripped through another intersection.

"Would you like me to?" Luciana turned and looked at her, pulling her eyes from the road in a way that made Helen's heart leap into her throat while simultaneously being one of the sexiest things she'd ever seen.

"Eye-eyes on the road!"

"Do I make you nervous?" Luciana purred, popping the brakes and taking a turn much faster than Helen would ever dream of doing.

"Yes!"

Luciana dropped to fifty-five, a flush in her cheeks and an apologetic expression taking up residence on her face.

"Sorry, I haven't really *driven* anything quite this powerful in a long time."

"I couldn't tell," Helen replied earnestly. "I mean, that was hot, and amazing, and sexy as hell but also *terrifying*."

"Fair enough, I apologize."

"That's like a racetrack, open highway, empty desert kind of thing for me," Helen felt guilty for spoiling Luciana's fun. "I'm–"

"Don't say sorry, Helen; you're enforcing a personal boundary and I am going to respect it," Luciana interrupted firmly. "I'm proud of you, you said setting boundaries was hard for you and here you're doing it."

Helen smiled hard enough she thought the sides of her mouth might split, her chest filled with a warmth that she wasn't sure she'd felt before Luciana, perhaps ever.

Yeah, you stupid broken girl, it's called a healthy relationship.

Helen ignored her inner demons and turned to look out the window at the warehouses and run-down apartments they were passing. The area was dilapidated to say the least, hardly the place you'd look for an exclusive club.

Then again, maybe that was the point.

Luciana turned down a narrow side-street, little more than an alley really, and brought the supercar down to a crawl.

"It says we're here, right?"

Helen followed her outstretched finger to the dash. The map did in fact indicate that they'd "reached their destination."

They pulled up under a streetlight, which shed a small circle of yellowish light on the cracked asphalt beneath them. They were in a slightly larger space now, used to either turn around or, more likely, to enter one of the roll-down doors that punctuated either side of the alleyway.

"This is probably it," Luciana nodded at two burly men lurking in the shadows near a nondescript metal door with no visible handle.

The two men were massive, with blocky, body-builder frames and tailored suits. Neither had hair, and both sported sprawling head and hand tattoos.

"Wait," Helen reached out but Luciana had already opened her door and stepped out into the night.

"What if they're like …serial killers or mobsters or something," Helen grumbled to herself and extricated herself from the vehicle as well.

"Good evening gentlemen," Luciana's voice was disarming as Helen hurried to catch up. "I believe you'll need these?"

She produced the two heavy coins just as Helen fell into place at her left side. She finally got a good look at the discs, which featured a double-headed eagle engraved on each side, as Luciana handed them over.

"Welcome to Psilo," the man on the left, a towering six-foot-four monster of a man, smiled and held out his hand as the other tapped a pattern on the door. "I'll take your keys."

Luciana dropped her keyfob in the man's hand after receiving her coins back, then smiled as the door eased silently open. The loud wub-wub-wub of heavy bass disturbed the still air, and green flashing lights illuminated a hallway ahead of them.

"Come along," Luciana whispered, placing a hand on Helen's back and propelling her gently forward.

Helen stepped into the dim hallway and immediately the temperature rose by one or two degrees. The door shut behind them and Helen took a moment to look at Luciana, who was right behind her.

"Go," she urged. "I'm right here."

"Luciana, that car was like a bazillion dollars, you just *gave* that dude the keys?"

"Clubs like this don't fuck things up, otherwise they don't last."

"Ok, well, you go first."

Luciana sidled past her to take the lead.

Helen breathed a little easier following her partner into the unknown, but still felt out of place. At least until they rounded a corner and were faced with an industrial steel staircase leading downward. The music was louder here, and Helen recognized a remix of a house favorite of hers from her sophomore year of college.

I wonder what else will be the same.

Luciana braved the stairs first, with Helen hovering behind her. When they reached the bottom, the stairs opened up onto a large metal catwalk that surrounded a huge open room. The catwalk held tables, all welded in place to the grating below them, around which dozens of patrons were drinking, laughing, and conversing. The real eye-catcher though was the dancefloor down below. A spiral metal staircase descended into the absolute chaos of hundreds of rich, beautiful people gyrating to heavy electronica being blasted from a wall of speakers at least twenty feet high.

The DJ, a woman with short, bright-blue hair, and a pair of sunglasses, was manning a table of buttons, knobs, and instruments at the far end of the dance floor and her image was displayed on several flatscreens around the room alongside the words 'DJ Rylie Flux.'

The music poured over Helen the moment she stepped across the threshold, and she felt a tug on her heart and mind like she'd felt in the staircase back at Casa De Rosas.

"There's magic here," Luciana warned. "You need to be careful."

Helen didn't care; she could already feel the bass in her blood and the blaze from a dozen lasers and strobes were blending together in a symphony of light and sounds.

"Helen," Luciana shook her, drawing Helen's gaze. "*Be careful*. This place is Fae, remember what I told you."

"Relax, Luci," Helen shouted over the music. "I know my way around a club!"

"Helen, I'm serious. I want you to stay up here, off the dance floor, ok? I'm going to go find Tetiana."

She was gone before Helen could answer, leaving her awkward and alone amidst the city's elite.

She could feel herself pulsing in and out of clarity, an effect that made her feel simultaneously wide awake and a bit tipsy. Her hips and shoulders both swayed to the beat, but she kept herself from getting too wild.

Luciana said stay here.

Do we always have to do what she says?

Afraid you'll have fun?

"Hey," a man's voice, silky and with a light eastern european accent, caught her attention. "I'm Phillipe."

She turned at the man's words—and his unexpected touch at her waist. He was tall, maybe 5'11", and of stocky build. Long locks of wavy black hair hung to his shoulders and provided a stark counterpoint to his emerald eyes. Helen took in the sight of his black vest—he wore no shirt underneath it—and matching slacks and shoes. He was in great shape, like a football player, and sweat from dancing shone on his pale skin.

"I said, I'm Phillipe," he extended a hand toward her. "Can I have your name?"

Yummy.

Names have power.

"Ellen," she lied, shaking his hand.

He took her hand and kissed the back of it, but something flashed in his eyes. Was it surprise? Disappointment?

"A beautiful name for a beautiful girl."

"I-I'm sorry," Helen caught a whiff of strong, bold perfume that fogged her mind further. "I'm actually here with someone–"

"Where is he?" Phillipe laughed. "Surely it is a crime to leave such a beautiful woman alone.

"Or she," a woman interjected as she stepped around Helen's side. "Don't be so conservative, Phillipe."

"I'm Katja," the woman stepped up and kissed Helen on both cheeks before she could think to react. "A pleasure."

Katja was short, thick, and equally eastern European. The two were cut from the same cloth, though she was wearing a strappy black lace bodysuit with crimson red trimmings and a pair of black leather platform shoes.

"Hi, uh, I'm–"

"Ellen," the woman purred. "I overheard."

Helen swallowed a lump in her throat.

"Why don't you have a drink with us," Katja nodded at a now empty table. "We'll wait for your friend together."

"S-sure," Helen smiled, allowing herself to be led to the high-top.

They no sooner took their places around the industrial metal table, than a young man wearing nothing but a pair of black latex shorts and a black bunny mask appeared beside them.

"May I get you anything?

Helen tried to cover her surprise at seeing a gorgeous twink in underwear as a waiter, and was glad the other two ordered first.

"Three Brisbane Gold Line Martinis, two dirty," Katja spoke as though she was talking to a servant, her disdain for the waiter dripping from her words. "Three sugar cubes and…Oh, how do you take your martinis, *Ellen*?"

Not this fancy, usually?

"Erm, I guess like yours," Helen smiled at the waiter to make up for Katja's rudeness. "Not dirty though for me, please."

"Neat," Katja smiled broadly as the man stepped away. "So you don't fuck around."

"And she's sweet to the *help*," Phillipe smirked, looking back and forth from Helen to the waiter. "*Adorable*. You must be new here."

"I-I just think everyone deserves some kindness," Helen stammered. "No matter their job, you know?"

"Too right you are," Katja laughed. "But the boys in latex *like* being spoken down to."

"What?"

"The waiters, the waitresses, all of the staff," she explained. "They're ah…color-coded so to speak."

"Latex like degradation, lace like praise," Phillipe continued, pointing out another young man in a similar outfit. "Clubwear is tougher, you have to actually know the colors. Blues like it when customers get handsy, pinks are available for…rent, yellows are hands off, red are–"

"Reds are reserved for the VIP section," Katja's eyes flashed brightly as she struck a pose in her own outfit. "So naturally we have to be a bit tight-lipped, you understand."

"Yes, of course," Helen was saved by the return of their waiter.

"It took you long enough," Phillipe snapped.

"Pathetic," Katja sighed as the man handed out their drinks as well as a small porcelain saucer that had three sugar cubes on it.

The pair looked at Helen expectantly.

"Don't look at me," she said cooly. "I won't speak to him, he's beneath my station."

The man bit his lip in a way that could only mean one thing, then dropped a quick bow and made his exit.

"See, fun isn't it?"

"Yeah," she accepted her drink, then paused when the two each took their sugar cubes and Katja slid the dish over to her.

Fuck.

Woohoo!

Now that she could get a closer look, she understood the strangeness of ordering sugar cubes with their drinks. A small but clear blue smiley face was printed on the top of the sugar cube.

They wouldn't really just order LSD off the menu.

It'll be fun finding out.

"You *do* partake, don't you Ellen?"

"Of course she does, Katja," Phillipe scoffed. "Why else would she come to Psilo, you can *drink* anywhere."

"Of course," Helen tried to stifle the part of her that was throwing an absolute party, to heed the fading voice of caution in her mind.

After all, you're still up here, you're still doing what Luciana told you to.

What your boss told you.

"She's not my *boss*," Helen huffed under her breath.

"What was that love?" Phillipe leaned closer, the alcohol on his breath becoming apparent. "Hard to hear over the music."

"Nothing," Helen made up her mind "Cheers!"

She raised her sugar cube, then popped the whole thing in her mouth.

Any trace of hesitation was rapidly erased by the treacly sweet of the sugar cube, which she washed down with a sip of her drink. The vodka was incredibly smooth. It had a clean finish that let her taste the quality, and it had none of the harshness she was used to.

It tasted like money.

"Oh," she took another sip. "Wow that's good."

"You're in Psilo, gorgeous," Katja ran a finger down her arm. "Everything's good."

Had Katja always been that close to her? Was the table shrinking?

Helen smiled and—to her credit—didn't shirk away despite the coolness of the woman's touch.

"So I hear."

"It's your first time, is it not?"

"How could you tell?" she answered Phillipe's question. "Do I look that out of place?"

"Not at all," he grinned in a hungry manner "You look delicious. You seem a bit…ah, *delicate* though."

Helen's hackles raised defensively against her will and better judgment.

"Meaning?"

"Oh, do not take offense, please," Phillipe took a heavy sip of his martini. "I'm sure you've had more experience in more standard clubs, the atmosphere here can be a bit more intense."

"More intimate," Katja was now standing directly beside her. "With more…options."

"I'm familiar with options," Helen heard herself answer cockily. "And intimacy."

"Is that so?" Katja purred.

"It's just I'm waiting on–"

"Your friend, yes," Phillipe looked around. "Perhaps they've lost track of you?"

"Or maybe we know them, we could help you look."

"I'm here with Tetiana," Helen drained half of her martini to keep from betraying her lie.

Katja recoiled as though she'd been bit by a snake, meanwhile Phillipe grinned even wider.

"Is that so?"

"Yes," Helen stumbled. "Well, *for* Tetiana. My g-girlfriend and I are–"

"Well you won't find her up here," Katja grabbed her hand and pulled her away from the table and toward the stairs. "Come on, she'll be in the back."

Phillipe finished his martini and stood to follow.

"With the reds."

Chapter Nine

Fuck.

By the time Helen made it to the bottom of the stairs—still hand in hand with Katja—she could feel the first effects of the LSD in her system.

This shouldn't be happening yet.

She recalled Luciana's warning that Fae energy could warp and enhance substances, and she grimaced. She couldn't feel nervous for more than a moment though, as a feeling of overwhelming euphoria hit her like a wave.

She stepped down onto the dance floor with a wide grin plastered on her face and faced the crush of writhing, gyrating bodies. Arms and legs blended together and the beat of the music was visible as pulses of light and energy that flickered out between the glowing beams of the lasers overhead.

"Come on," Katja tugged gently.

Helen pulled her hand free and spun in a slow circle as a row of glowing green mushrooms was projected from the DJ booth all around the perimeter of the dance floor. The mushrooms pulsed, then flashed to red, yellow, and finally blue, eventually morphing through the entire rainbow before flickering out again.

"Holy shit," she breathed, her voice sounding distant and distorted.

"It gets better," Katja whispered in her ear, before tugging her into the crowd.

Within seconds, they were deep in the masses. Katja's arms were in the air as she danced mere inches away in front of Helen, and Phillipe did the same just behind her. She could feel their combined bodyheat as a sort of pressure on her skin, setting her nerves on fire and her skin tingling.

The beat was hard, fast, and heavy. Time seemed to slow as Katja pressed her sizable rear end against Helen's hips, leaning until her back was against her chest, and running her hands up and down Helen's thighs as she swayed.

"So does your girlfriend share?" she asked over the music.

Helen looked at the woman's slender, doll-like face in the flashing light from the strobes above. Her eyes reflected sparkling neon green and her dark lipstick was an open invitation. Sweat shone on her high cheekbones and her expression begged for Helen's attention.

"No," she forced herself to answer, despite an ache between her legs and a pounding in her chest. ""'S-sorry, we haven't talked about tha–"

"Shame," Katja's voice resonated in Helen's lungs as she pressed back harder. "We'll have to ask when we find her."

Helen felt Phillipe's hands on her waist and was surprised at how ok she felt with it. The pressure of expectations lifted, she lost herself in the music and her partners. Time blurred and she oscillated back and forth between dancing along, with Katja and Phillipe, and with a thousand other faceless men and women who shared the floor with them. The longer she danced, the more she lost herself, until her hair was slick with sweat and her heartbeat pounded in her ears.

"Hey stranger."

She whirled around, a sloppy grin on her face, and found Katja standing there with Phillipe and another of the wait staff. This one was a tall latina woman wearing a french maid outfit and a cherry-red ball gag. No, not tall, Helen realized, noting the seven-inch, high-angle stilettos. The girl was holding a small round mirror in one hand like a serving platter. The thing had heavy silver trim polished to a shine, and two long, perfectly straight lines of snowy white powder.

"My treat," Katja shouted over the din, holding out a rolled up hundred dollar bill. "Phillipe and I wanted to see if you were ready to come back to the *real* party yet?"

Helen was too far gone to even think twice.

She grabbed the bill and held it to the mirror, catching a look at her reddened cheeks and blown-out pupils as she did so. It was a face she recognized, one she'd seen a thousand times on a thousand different nights since leaving home. A trill of fear tried to penetrate her foggy mind, but it couldn't break through the manic high she was swirling in.

The powder burned as it entered her nose, it tingled and numbed and shot fire directly into her mind. She rubbed her nostril with the back of her hand as she handed back the bill and watched Katja snort the remaining line.

Clarity hit her like a brick as the cocaine worked its own brand of magic and intensified the extra sensory input from the LSD in her system. Everything had hard edges and lines like a comic book page, but the colors leaked out between them like a glow in the dark water painting.

"She's wearing red," Helen noted, her words rushed.

Katja smiled back, then grabbed Helen's hand firmly and dragged her through the press of bodies.

A few minutes later, the pair emerged from the crowd at the other end of the dance floor. A purple velvet rope sectioned off a small area around a peculiar black door. The door was old and wooden, and seemed utterly out of place in the otherwise industrial, techy surroundings of the club. Moreover, it was flanked by two massive men in dark suits. A small crowd of people was waiting in some semblance of a line, but there didn't look to be any movement.

Helen picked out the faces of a few movie stars, a couple of men and women she'd seen in news articles over the years, and other recognized but unknown faces, in the line waiting to get in, but Katja stepped past them heedless of any protests.

"Hey Ricky," she winked as one of the men reached over and unclipped the rope, allowing Katja to step through with Helen in tow.

"Easy," the man rumbled, putting a hand on Helen's chest that felt as immovable as stone.

"She's with me, Ricky," Katja laughed, then leaned closer. "And she's here for Tetiana."

The man paused, then removed his hand and allowed Helen through before reclipping the rope behind her.

"Enjoy your time with us, ladies."

The second bouncer reached out and wrapped a tattooed hand around the heavy bronze handle of the door, pulling it open for the two women as they approached. The entryway was obscured by a gauzy purple curtain that was flecked with sparkling gold, which Helen allowed herself to be led through.

The cloth was soft, and they stepped through several flowing layers of it before emerging on the other side.

Helen planted her heels in shock, eliciting an amused chuckle from Katja, who seemed content to bask in Helen's reaction.

This room was made of stone, and seemed far removed from the lights and sounds of the dance floor behind her. Unlike the industrial club scene behind her, this room was a much more organic room. The walls were made of rough cut blocks of stone, and the floor was multileveled. There were hot tubs sunken into the floor haphazardly around the room, as well as massive piles of cushions, plush sitting areas with low tables, ornate glass hookah pipes, and massive communal mattresses.

And naked or scantily clad people *everywhere*.

Moans and grunts of pleasure accompanied sexual acts that ranged from the vanilla across the gamut of sexuality and kink. In one corner, a woman was being shared between five men, and on another couch a man was being flogged by a person clad entirely in latex. She watched as a woman in a pink negligee fed strawberries to a middle aged woman reclining nude on a comfortable looking chaise lounge, then found her eyes traveling to an orgy of women frolicking on a broad mattress inset into the floor.

Food, sex, and drink surrounded her, in a cacophony of sinful pleasure.

"Katja–"

Helen's mouth snapped shut as a waiter wearing a pair of red and white briefs was yanked down off of one of the narrow paths between the play areas. The man who'd grabbed him forced him onto his knees, then gripped him by his hair before reaching for his fly.

"Red is for *free use*," Katja snaked a hand up Helen's thigh. "We're *literally* asking for it."

She intertwined her fingers into Helen's and smiled again, her teeth shockingly white and flickering between sharp points and normal flat human teeth.

Gotta be the acid.

Does it?

Helen felt heat rising in her body as she looked out over the room.

Free use.

Her eyes landed on a pair of women who were balancing a pane of glass between their backs. The glass was being used as a table to hold drinks and a pair of hookahs being shared by a small group of men wearing only slacks and opera masks. One of the men took a long toke of the water pipe and blew a cloud of glittering pink smoke directly into one of the women's faces and she smiled, but said nothing.

"Come on," Katja looped an arm around Helen. "Let's go see Tetiana."

Oh you fucked up now.

They walked through clouds of sweet-smelling smoke that tickled her nose, winding their way between deviants toward the back of the room. When Tetiana finally came into view, there could be no mistaking her.

She was, somehow, even more attractive than Helen had seen in her extensive collection of porn videos. Styxx. Her blond hair stood out from the black leather "bus driver" cap she wore. She had a corset on, but it left her breasts bare. She was wearing black leather gloves and a pair of mid-thigh patent leather boots—and nothing else.

She was seated on what could only be called a throne.

It was made of stone—or looked like it—with a plump purple cushion on the seat and back. It was set in the center of a low dais which was adorned with a half-dozen submissive men and women. Her stable of worshippers—for their body language was that of the most devout follower—all wore matching black leather collars along with their lingerie. She watched as Tetiana extended one of her heeled boots absentmindedly and one of the men below her gripped it before running his tongue up the side of it hungrily. Styxx laughed and kicked the man down again before turning to speak to–

"Luciana," Helen blurted out, garnering a look from Katja.

"Your girlfriend?"

"Yeah."

Helen couldn't take her eyes off Luciana, whose skin was sparkling in the dim lighting of the lounge. For a moment, the woman had a pair of angelic feathered wings, but they disappeared just as quickly. Next, Helen would swear her height was fluctuating wildly by as much as a foot.

In fact, everywhere she looked the room was swirling with colors and sounds that were igniting her senses like wildfire.

"Well, come on," Katja tugged, her free hand fingering the leather collar she wore. "Introduce me."

"Mistress," Katja's whole body shivered as they approached the throne and she dropped to her knees, dragging Helen with her. "Look what I found for you–"

"My sister's pretty little pet," Tetiana exclaimed brightly, standing up and brushing past a visibly stunned Luciana. "I'm so glad my little birdies found you."

"What the hell are you doing here?" Luciana hissed, taking a step forward.

"Sister," Tetiana snapped, stepping down the dias, but not turning back to look at Luciana. "Don't be *rude*. She's welcome in my house."

"Her name is Ellen, mistress," Katja spoke, only to be silenced by a raised finger from Tetiana.

"Good girl," Tetiana praised the woman, who practically shook with elation. "Go play."

Helen scrambled to her feet as Katja let go of her hand. She stood awkwardly as her teen sex idol walked slowly around her, scrutinizing her head to toe.

"She's…" Tetiana turned a raised eyebrow to Luciana. "Not like us. An interesting choice, sister."

"Excuse us for a moment," Luciana found her voice again.

She stepped over to Helen and steered her not so gently off a few feet from the throne, waiting until their backs were turned to lean in close and catch Helen's gaze.

"What are you *thinking*?" her voice held more concern than anything else, and Helen was mesmerized by blue swirls of worry that flowed through her eyes and across her lips.

"Helen, are you…?" Luciana snapped her fingers in front of Helen's face, the sound waves visible as tiny sparkles of licorice flavored noise. "Oh honey, what did you take?"

"Just the fun stuff," Helen found herself grinning.

Luciana looked afire, her skin radiant and her outfit clinging desperately to her toned, well-muscled build in a way that was turning the already aroused Helen to jelly.

"You know," Helen set her arms on Luciana's hips and tugged her closer. "I can't help but notice that everyone else seems to be having more fun than us."

She could feel waves of energy, a sort of magnetic tug and flow radiating off of her lover and rocking through her own body in response.

"God you're beautiful," Helen murmured, leaning in to press herself against Luciana in a tight embrace.

"And you're high as a kite," Luciana pulled back slightly, revealing an oil slick shine of purples and greens dancing through her curly hair.

She leaned forward and planted a kiss on Helen's cheek that spread warmth in a ripple along her entire body.

"We'll have plenty of time to play when you're–"

Helen interrupted her with a deep kiss, wrapping her arms around Luciana's neck and lifting herself up to wrap her legs around her as well. Luciana's hands instinctively moved to cradle her rear, and her lips responded in kind.

"It's Tetiana's magic," Luciana mumbled through their dancing tongues. "She makes people around her–"

"Horny?"

Luciana laughed, pulling back while Helen nibbled at her neck.

"Yes, she's a succubus, she feeds on erotic energy."

"I know what I want," Helen insisted, pouting at Luciana's words. "Succubus or not."

"Honey, I warned you this place was dangerous. There's magic working on your mind," Luciana's smile was blue and white, and cooled the temperature of their embrace.

"Fine," Helen stepped down, scooting back from Luciana and crossing her arms as the coldness of Luciana's rebuke lingered on her skin.

"Hel–"

"It's fine," Helen shivered, trying to ignore the blues and purples swirling across her body and leaving her feeling chilled. "You're right."

"Aww," Tetiana crowed from her dais. "Your pet is sad. We can't have that out here in the playroom, why don't you two come to the back with me?"

"Good idea."

Luciana followed Tetiana as she headed to a darkened corner behind the throne, with Helen trailing a few steps behind.

It's starting already, she doesn't want you.

"Shut up."

Helen ignored the shadows jeering at her as she followed the women to a door hidden by darkness. It opened at Tetiana's approach, and stayed that way long enough for the trio to pass through.

She was surprised to find herself in an open grove, with the starry sky overhead and no walls whatsoever. Instead, there were moss-covered rocks, a bubbling stream, and dark tall trees as far as she could see in any direction. The grove itself was a mix of soft grasses and wild herbs, all situated within a rough, circular patch of soccer ball sized mushrooms.

"Have a seat, Ellen," Tetiana waved at a nearby stump, beside which sat a low table. "While my sister and I talk."

Helen smiled weakly, goosebumps all along her legs and arms as she felt herself shrinking away from the darkness around them. The trees creaked in an unfelt wind, the stars overhead seemed like angry eyes filled with judgment, and even the brook was whispering doubt into her mind.

You're not good enough.

We told you so.

Matter of time.

"Baby, are you ok?"

Luciana's question went unanswered as it melded with the conversations in Helen's mind.

"How 'bout some tea?" Tetiana's voice cut through the chaos and a fine porcelain tea set appeared on the table next to Helen, complete with a small cup of dark green, gently steaming liquid.

"N-no thank you."

"*Drink,*" Tetiana insisted. "It's only polite, and it'll calm your nerves."

Helen obediently lifted the cup, ignoring the rattle of the saucer from her unsteady grip, and took a gulp of the scalding liquid. It was earthy but smooth, with layer after layer of flavor.

"Thisss isss gooood," she slurred, her words feeling foreign as they left her mouth.

Helen blinked as her vision started to blur. She could see Luciana and Tetiana arguing—yelling at each other in fact—but all she could hear was her own heartbeat as the whole world suddenly tilted sideways. She blinked again and found herself laying on the impossibly soft ground, the empty teacup rolling in front of her, and the sky rushing down to meet her.

Then nothing.

Chapter Ten

"Helen, baby, wake up," Luciana's voice was fighting hard against the foggy darkness, but it seemed to be winning. "Helen, you're going to feel groggy for a moment, but the feeling should pass."

Light joined the sounds, and Luciana's face—marred by obvious concern—swam into view.

"Wha-what happened?"

Details became clearer and she could see that she was in a forest, looking up at the pink-tinged sky.

What the fuck am I doing outside?

Her memory returned in flashes as she sat up, her head pounding and her mouth dry.

"My darling sister–"

"You needed a nap," a colder, yet still familiar voice interrupted. "You were spiraling and I had no intention of watching it."

"Tetiana," Luciana growled, moving away.

"You're going to tell me I'm *wrong?*" the voice insisted. "Besides, she's fine."

Helen made it up to a sitting position and took stock of herself. She was still wearing her clubwear, as were Luciana and Tetiana. She was seated on the plush moss she'd fallen asleep on, but there was no sign of the chair, the side table stump, or her tea set. Instead, Luciana and her sister were both lounging on chairs that looked to be made from living willow branches, while Helen had been sleeping on what amounted to a bed of moss and flowers.

"You just *left me on the ground*?" she asked indignantly.

"You are privileged to enter this grove because of your association with my sister," Tetiana cautioned. "Do not dismiss or disrespect that fact."

"She meant no offense."

Helen struggled to her feet, her arms and legs heavy as lead.

"Why do I feel like I got roofied?"

"You needed to sleep off the substances in your system if we were going to have a productive conversation—something that we apparently *must* do," Tetiana drawled.

"Tetiana, I told you already," Luciana sighed. "I know you're situated well here, and I'm not asking you to intervene directly, but if you could just use your sight–"

"The Smiling Man doesn't play by the *rules*, sister. It won't be you he guts if he finds out I helped you try to kill him."

"So you're scared."

"Fuck yes I'm scared," Tetiana scoffed. "There are rumors swirling out there that he's strong enough to fight an elder now, or nearly so."

"He wouldn't kill an oracle," Luciana insisted. "Some things are still sacred."

"How would you know? Aside from a few brief forays, you've been holed up in that mansion for decades."

"Hello," Helen waved her hands. "I'd like to be clued in a bit, if you don't mind."

Or you could go back to the party.

Now that was fun.

"I'm sorry, Helen," Luciana waved and a third chair appeared, as well as a pitcher of chilled water and a glass on another end table stump.

"I thought you couldn't use your magic in other people's, whatever," Helen sat. "Their fortress of solitude or lair or bat cave."

"Sisters are different," the two women spoke in perfect unison.

Helen rolled her eyes, feeling ill used.

"You should hydrate, you've been asleep for quite a while."

"What's quite a while?"

"Three days, but you were partying for a week, so that hardly seems like a bad trade."

"I was partying for a week?" Helen repeated dumbly. "That's not possible, we got here *tonight*."

"She's still learning," Luciana explained, looking at Tetiana. "I haven't told her about fairy rings yet."

"The mushroom lights," Helen realized, thinking back to the dance floor. "So all those people have been–"

"No no," Tetiana laughed. "I can't have famous folks going missing for weeks at a time without explanation. My thralls seek out patrons who are susceptible and—no offense—no one is likely to miss."

"Thralls?"

"Literal thralls, people who are addicted to her and will carry out her every whim. It's a defense mechanism, as well as a way to feed."

"Why throw a neverending rave in the first place?"

"As she said, I feed on it, I subsist on pleasure in every form."

The woman's grin was wicked and Helen felt herself flushing with desire against her will.

"What's happening to me?" Helen shook her head, blushing against the heat in her cheeks. "Why do I suddenly feel...?"

"*Aroused*?"

"Yes, stop it," she scowled, even as her thighs clenched.

"Your loss."

The feeling faded, but left Helen feeling a bit...cheap.

"Remember I told you that we grow, evolve, take new forms and abilities? Well, Tetiana's current form is that of a succubus, one of the Fae forms that deals with humanity the most...directly."

“I thought she was an oracle?” Helen crossed her arms, feeling less cocky, and more exposed, in her outfit by the moment. “Isn’t that why we came here?”

“You’ve been spilling secrets,” Tetiana feigned shock, clutching at non-existent pearls. “Naughty, naughty.”

“She is.”

“I am,” Tetiana agreed. “I retain the Sight. It’s a gift I was chosen to carry, and it is mine until the end of my days, no matter what form I choose to take.”

“So,” Helen narrowed her eyes. “What the hell are we supposed to do? How do we escape The Smiling Man?”

“You don’t,” Tetiana’s reply was flippant, and accompanied by a careless wave of her hand.

“Then you’ve already looked,” Luciana accused. “You’ve already seen our fates?”

“You know it doesn’t work like that…but I have seen *some* things, yes,” she agreed. “I’m warning you, most of it isn’t particularly pretty.”

“I’m a dragon hunter, sister, that hasn’t been news to me for centuries.”

"Your best bet is hallowed ground," Tetiana sipped her drink. "But you already knew that, so why don't you ask me what you're actually looking for."

"*Can* he be killed?"

"That's beyond my power to see, I'm sorry."

"Will Helen be ok?"

Silence.

"Tetiana," Luciana glanced sidelong at Helen. "How do I keep her safe?"

"I will not reveal another's fate," Tetiana turned toward Helen. "Not without her permission."

"But–"

"It is *law*."

Another icy silence.

"So, mortal," Tetiana took on the tiniest hint of pity. "Would you like to know what happens to you? How you die? *When* you die?"

Helen met Luciana's pleading gaze.

Yes.

No.

Why bother?

"No," she announced firmly. "No, I don't."

"Helen!"

“Very well.”

“Helen,” Luciana stood half in shock and half in anger, then approached her and brought her voice to a harsh whisper. “What are you thinking?”

“If your sister told you it was safer for you to leave me, would you?”

Luciana’s eyes widened but she said nothing.

“Yes or no, I know you can’t lie–”

“Yes, I would.”

“Then I don’t want to know.”

“This is so far past reckless, Helen,” she insisted. “You could get hurt, get killed, *worse*.”

“*I’m* not immortal,” Helen shot back. “And frankly, I’m surprised to be here as it is.”

“That’s not funny.”

“I’m not laughing.”

Helen tried to ignore the smirk on Tetiana’s face, but she couldn’t help feeling a flush in her cheeks as this unexpected standoff with her lover failed to resolve.

“Ok, I’m sorry, you’re right,” Luciana pinched the bridge of her nose. “It is your decision to make.”

"How nice for me," Helen's words came out snarkier than she'd intended.

"Helen, I'm trying to keep you safe because I care about you," Luciana's hackles were raised.

"Ok, but I'm *so* far out of my depth here," Helen's hands raised up in frustration. "I'm some pesky clueless mortal, you're yo-yoing back and forth between treating me like a child and pretending I'm an adult–"

"Because I don't want you getting stoned in an unfamiliar sex club while a monster is hunting us!?"

"Yes!"

"Helen–"

"I'm a grown up, I have agency," Helen stood. "As far as I can tell, you two are sorting out what happens next *for* me. You're certainly not looking to me for input."

"Helen, if you don't want to stay," Luciana's face was crestfallen.

"Ugh, damn it," Helen turned and paced. "I *do* want to stay, I really, *really* like you."

"But?"

"But I don't even know what we *are* at this point! Am I just a fun distraction? A blip in the endless timeline of your life? Is this a real relationship with a real future—are you going to get bored and drop me off somewhere along the way?"

"Tetiana, can we have a moment please?"

"Certainly," Tetiana drained her glass with a smile, then snapped her fingers and disappeared with a loud, sharp, whip-like *crack*.

"What do *you* want us to be?" Luciana stood as well, approaching Helen and placing her hands on her waist.

The woman's eyes were captivating, her smell intoxicating, and her earnest, genuine expression made keeping her walls up impossible.

"I want to…I want to date you," Helen admitted. "I want us to be an item, a thing, give this an actual shot. I…I've fucked up too many good *things* by treating them like good *times*, and I don't want that with you."

"I want the same," Luciana looked relieved. "This isn't going to be a cakewalk, hell this is about as complicated as a relationship can get, but I'd like to give it a real shot."

"So, equal footing," Helen half smiled. "Just a gal and her fairy princess?"

"Equal footing," Luciana nodded. "Partners, girlfriends, paramours, whatever the kids are saying these days."

"And you'll–"

"I'll respect your decisions, respect your choices," Luciana nodded, anticipating Helen's questions. "But I promised you I'd intervene if I had to, and I meant it."

Helen felt a pang of regret at having rashly accepted her terms and conditions.

"If you're going to get *hurt*, I can't just stand by," she insisted, her jaw set.

"Right," Helen sighed. "Y-you're right. I just…I've come to realize I feel helpless and unimportant when you're talking to other Fae."

"What do you mean?" Luciana wrapped her in a warm hug.

"Just that I don't know anything about anything," Helen's words were muffled. "And you talk over or around me, like I'm not really *there*—like I'm not part of the decision making process."

"I'm sorry," Luciana's hand reached up to the back of Helen's neck, firmly massaging the muscles there and releasing the knots that Helen hadn't realized had formed. "You're right, that's valid, and I'll do a better job of explaining things going forward—and making sure you feel like a valued part of the conversation."

"Do you have any idea of how sexy–"

And terrifying.

"–it is for me to be able to have a rational, healthy, productive conversation with my girlfriend?"

"Shouldn't that be sort of a bare minimum expectation?" Luciana laughed.

"You would think," Helen shrugged.

Unless the problem is you, and not them…not her.

"Helen," Luciana's embrace tightened. "I need to talk to my sister some more…do you want to stay?"

"Um," she hesitated. "Is it…did you want to catch up or? If it's personal, I can step out–"

"Some of it will be fairly personal, yes," Luciana held her out at arm's length. "Some of it will be about us, about our next steps. Do you want to be here, to erm, express what you'd like?"

Helen felt suddenly very awkward. She'd just thrown a fit to be included and yet—she realized with terrified frustration—she really didn't have a *clue* what to do next.

"I t-trust you," she stuttered. "I know you'll keep us safe, if you can."

"So then, do you want to stay?"

"I think I'd rather go back to the party, if that's ok."

"Helen, of course it is," Luciana gave her a sad smile—one that recognized her trauma response for what it was. "I will not, *should not,* control what you do, or where you go. Just be safe, ok?"

"And you'll come get me though, right?" Helen gulped. "You'll take me with you when it's time to leave?"

"I won't leave without you, I promise."

"Come here, little bird," Tetiana's voice broke the intimacy of the moment. "I have a gift for you."

Helen turned, breaking her embrace from Luciana, and eyed the oracle warily.

"A gift?"

"Yes, a gift free of debt or entanglements," Tetiana's smile was as sharp and wicked as her over-long incisors. "A homecoming present for my sister, of sorts."

Helen stepped forward, her heart pounding in her chest as she approached the woman. She couldn't help but drink in the raw sexuality that Tetiana exuded. Her plump curves, her silk-smooth skin, her sizable bust, impossibly perky, even her delicate, charming, youthful face screamed fertility and desire.

"I save this for *special* guests," Tetiana purred, holding a hand out, palm up.

Her hand began to glow, a faint green light emanating from it that grew until it was nearly too bright to look at. The trio cast strange shadows on the trees as the light concentrated into the woman's palm.

"Give me your hand."

Helen looked over at Luciana, who gave her a tiny nod of encouragement, then held her hand out. Tetiana reached forward, then wrapped her hand around

Helen's wrist. The skin below her hand started to tingle, then ache like a strong sunburn, before finally returning to normal as the light faded.

Tetiana removed her hand, revealing an intricate, winding tattoo around Helen's wrist. Bold black lines curved and swirled in a three inch wide band that wrapped all the way around. Stylized clusters of flowers emerged delicately from a plethora of tiny leaves and stems that wove across her skin with mesmerizing complexity.

"Uh–"

The ink flashed a muted green, then faded until it had all but disappeared, leaving only the faintest disturbance on her otherwise unblemished skin.

"You now bear my mark," Tetiana explained. "A symbol that will be recognizable to all Fae, and to my mortal thralls as well. This will afford you the full benefits of my clubs, including safe haven, food, drink, and any other form of…pleasure, that you may desire."

Helen didn't know what to say.

"It may also help you in your interactions with our kind, though—as your kind likes to say—your mileage may vary."

Helen cracked a smile at the idiom, still lost in contemplation about her new magical accessory.

"Does every Fae have a mark?"

"Every Fae *can* have a mark," Luciana interjected. "Once they become powerful enough. It's sort of like a signature, and it confers different things, different statuses, and privileges based on the Fae who grants it."

"I'm not sure what to–"

"Just say thank you," Luciana smiled.

Obviously, idiot.

"Right s-sorry, thank you so much Tetiana, I'm so grateful for–"

Tetiana raised a finger, smiling brightly.

"You can pay me back with a small favor," she grinned wickedly.

"Oh," Helen was surprised, expecting some version of Luciana's 'there is no debt' comment. "Ok?"

She looked over as Luciana's back stiffened and her eyes narrowed.

"Sister…"

"Relax," Tetiana laughed before turning back to Helen.

"Go enjoy yourself, please," Tetiana smiled warmly. "You've chosen a hard road, better to revel while you can."

Helen knew a dismissal when she heard one.

"Right," she stepped up on her tiptoes and gave Luciana a quick kiss before turning around to face the woods. "So how do I–"

She was mid-sentence when she felt the ground yanked out from under her.

She stumbled forward, her vision blinking in and out of blackness, and found herself suddenly standing in the same darkened corner of the dancefloor she'd left before.

"Ma'am."

The same heavyset, musclebound bouncer from before was looking at her with newfound respect.

"Ricky, right?"

He nodded, with a smile in his eyes that didn't reach his stoic face.

"Tetiana said, um, I don't know what I'm…doing."

"Treat the club and staff as if they were yours, ma'am," he gave her a little nod. "Your pleasure and your protection here are our promise."

Free reign?

Free reign!

"Thanks, Ricky," she smiled timidly, but her excitement was growing by the second.

She walked toward the velvet rope, which the man opened for her to pass through, and met the jealous gazes of the millionaires and famous faces waiting desperately in line.

"Hey, what makes *you* special," a tall blonde starlet she was passing looked down her perfect nose at Helen, fire in her eyes. "You're nobody."

"Babe," her boyfriend, a lean Italian man with a popped collar on a deep purple shirt and slicked back hair. "Chill."

But it was too late.

"Time to go."

Ricky's voice beside her made Helen jump—he could move pretty fucking quietly for a man of his size.

"What," the blonde sputtered in shock. "Do you know who I *am*?"

"Time. To. Go."

Another bouncer appeared from the crowd, moving to stand next to Ricky amidst a flurry of murmurs.

"We're moving," the woman's boyfriend grabbed her by the hand and started dragging her out of line.

"I've been waiting for four hours," the blonde shrieked. "Are you fucking kidding me?"

"You can leave quietly, or you can leave noisily," the new bouncer growled. "But you should know that noisy usually means messy."

Something in his tone conveyed a level of violence that sent a ripple down Helen's spine—along with a feeling of power, was this just for her?

"Quiet," the boyfriend yanked the girl's arm again. "We choose quiet, thank you."

The pair left in the company of the new bouncer, though the woman gave Helen an ugly stare until she disappeared around the edge of the crowd.

"My apologies," Ricky looked down at her. "Please let us know if you have any further trouble. We'll be keeping an eye on you as well."

With that the giant man stepped back to his position at the velvet rope and Helen turned back to the dance floor, ignoring the curious stares of the line beside her.

Chapter Eleven

Heavy bass rocked the crowd as Helen danced with a recklessness she'd never felt before. She tried to tamp down the building feeling of immortality and power but every beat of the music, every sweat drop that rolled down her back, every respectful nod from the staff, sent her higher above cloud nine.

She'd made her way close to the center of the dance floor, immersed in a crush of movement, heat, and sound that made it impossible to do anything *but* feel the energy. Her heart pulsed with the beat, her hands waved overhead, and she relished the unfelt touch of laserlights washing over her body from above.

Careful.

Fuck off.

"It looks like y'all are getting hot out there!"

The voice, magnified by the speakers, seemed to come from everywhere. It was soft, clear, and feminine, with a slight Scandinavian accent, and it was accompanied by a massive cheer from the crowd. Blue and white strobes flickered across the ceiling, giving the impression of a rolling thunderhead.

"Y'all know what time it is," Helen turned and finally realized it was the DJ speaking into a microphone. "If you're not tryna get wet, you better get the fuck off my floor!"

A triple air horn blared, followed by a magnified crackle of thunder that shook the room. A few people ran for the edges of the dance floor or toward the stairs leading upward, but most everyone stayed, their faces upturned.

The rolling sounds of thunder became less random, less chaotic, and slowly resolved into a familiar beat: *Thunderstruck* by AC/DC.

By the time the guitar faded in, the whole crowd was jumping in unison.

"Thunder," the chant shook the room. "Thunder, thunder."

Helen allowed herself to be swept up in the movement, bouncing on the balls of her feet and screaming at the top of her lungs with the crowd.

When Brian Johnson's voice broke the chant with the first few lyrics, he was accompanied by a sudden downpour as sprinklers in the ceiling activated—perfectly timed with a brilliant lightning flash of the strobes.

Helen was soaked in seconds, her hair whipping around as the crowd was driven to a frenzy.

Five minutes later, as the song came to an end, Helen found herself panting and her pulse roaring in her head.

We need a drink.

She looked around, trying to identify someone from the staff, and almost immediately made contact with a chiseled young man wearing latex shorts with a light blue trim and a matching blue bowtie. He was nearer to the stage, standing with his hands behind his back and scanning the crowd politely.

Helen pushed her way forward, navigating as gently as she could through the crush of bodies until she, too, was at the edge of the stage. She raised a finger to signal the young man's attention and was rewarded with an instantaneous response. His face went from dull but polite to bright and cheerful in a nanosecond and he stepped over to her immediately.

"Ya ma'am?"

"I need a drink," Helen leaned in to speak over the noise. "Some ice water, please."

Water?

Pathetic.

The man turned to leave, apparently unable to see Helen wrestling with herself, but just as he stepped away, she reached out and tapped his shoulder.

"Wait," she cleared her throat as he turned back expectantly. "Scratch that, um…"

What was it Katja ordered?

"I'll take a Beluga Gold Line Martini, with a twist and–"

Do it.

"A sugar cube."

Good girl.

"Right away, ma'am," he nodded, his demeanor unchanged from before.

Latex likes degradation, blue likes it when you're handsy.

She could practically hear Katja purring the words in her mind.

Helen reached out and grabbed the man by the chin, making sure he was looking her in the eyes, and reveling in the feeling of power that surged through her.

"And make it fucking snappy."

The man's eyes sparkled and his cheeks flushed.

"Ye's ma'a–"

"Get out of my sight."

She beamed as he scurried away, practically running to carry out her wishes.

"Nice."

Helen turned and found herself facing the stage. The DJ had stepped away from her gear and was now sitting on the edge of the stage a few feet away, her legs dangling over the edge and a bottle of water in her hands.

"Rylee," she held a hand out, her eyes unreadable through the dark lenses of her sunglasses.

"Ellen," Helen answered, taking her hand and shaking it gently.

"You're new here?"

"Yeah, how can everyone tell?"

"It's not like that," Rylee laughed. "Just that you seem to really *feel* the music. Lots of the people who come here don't care what I play, just that they're here where the 'it crowd' is."

"Well, I think it's fuckin' sick," Helen's voice was raised to cover the repetitive thumping bass of the track currently playing. "This set-up is insane."

"I designed it myself, so I'm glad you think so!"

"So then you know…" Helen nodded over toward the bouncers at the far end of the dance floor.

"Yeah me and Tetiana go way back," she laughed. "I was a siren in a past life, if you catch my drift. Music is my passion and—since it gives people pleasure—we're a natural fit."

"So you're…" Helen looked at her meaningfully.

"Yes," another beautiful laugh that seemed to echo in Helen's ears. "Which you get to know, since you're wearing *that*."

Rylee pointed at Helen's wrist.

"Right," she replied sheepishly.

"Look, this song is almost over but uh," she glanced at the sound equipment on the stage. "You got any requests?"

"Something hard," Helen answered immediately. "How 'bout *War Pigs*?"

"Sabbath? Fuck yeah," Rylee laughed. "You got a hell of a sense of humor asking for that in here."

Just like witches at black masses.

Helen watched as Rylee produced a small, pinky-finger sized gold cylinder, unscrewed the top, and pulled the cap off. The cap was connected to a thin metal rod that ended in a tiny spoon-like blade. Her mouth watered as Rylee dipped the tiny spoon into the cylinder, then lifted it up again with a small pile of white powder. She brought it to her nose and sniffed before shaking her head and smiling at Helen, who was watching her like a hawk.

"You want a bump?"

No.

"Hell yeah."

Helen stepped over as Rylee dipped the spoon in once more, this time holding it out for Helen to lean over. She used her pointer finger to block one nostril, and pulled the powder into her nose with a sharp inward breath. Immediately she felt the familiar sting and numbing of the cocaine, along with the electric rush of energy.

"Back to it," Rylee stowed the cylinder and stood before pointing at Helen. "*War Pigs* yeah?"

Helen nodded, rubbing her nose.

"Enjoy the party."

By the time the song ended and the first few notes of Black Sabbath roared out of the speakers, Helen could feel her blood tingling in her veins. She was *pumped*, full of energy, and buzzing for an outlet.

"Ma'am–"

She whirled around to find the waiter there.

"You took forever, I'm stunned I haven't died of old age."

"I'm sorry, I–"

"Shut up," Helen stepped close, really close, and ran a finger up the center of the man's prominent abs.

She took in the sight of the tray he held, sugarcube and all, and smiled. Helen popped the sugar cube into her mouth and followed it up by chugging the entirety of her martini.

"My fucking cup is empty," she set it back down heavier than she needed to. "Don't let it happen again."

"Yes ma'am," the man was visibly excited at her conduct.

"And don't think about helping anyone else," Helen pushed her boundaries, looking for a reaction. "Your services are mine tonight, you do what *I* say."

"Yes, of course ma'am," he smiled.

You're having too much fun with this.

No such thing.

Several martinis, and plenty of Ozzy Osbourne later, the whole fucking world was spinning.

Helen worked her way out of the crowd, leaning her back against the stage and bracing herself with her hands out wide, gripping the metal corner of the stage. She could feel her legs trembling and unsteady, her head was pounding, and her breath was short, and in spite of it all, she was beaming. She hadn't had a single truly cohesive thought in god knows how long, and she hadn't been this free since she'd left Texas A&M.

"Would the lady like another martini?" her personal waiter, who she'd named 'dog,' much to his pleasure, was standing there with another drink.

"Is this my fourth or fifth, Dog?"

"The lady's fifth."

"Whew," she lifted the glass and drained most of it, relishing the smoothness of the drink and cognizant of the fact that she could no longer taste the alcohol. "Thought I was losing count."

"Should I get another?"

"I need an upper," Helen shook her head, trying to get them to un-blur.

"Uh…"

"Can you get powder?"

"Well–"

"Coke, Dog, can you get me cocaine?"

"Oh, yeah, I mean, yes ma'am."

"I want that," she finished her martini. "And another of these."

Take it easy.

Too late for that.

Helen closed her eyes, leaning more heavily against the stage as she struggled to keep her feet.

Lights, sounds, and colors had long since started blending, and she hadn't been able to tell *exactly* what was real or not for the past…hour? Two? That said, the drink was rapidly overcoming the acid and she was quickly hitting a brick wall.

Even with her eyes closed, she could see amorphous blobs and streaks of color, which bobbed and wove into a complex tapestry of vivid light.

"Ma'am?"

Helen cracked an eye and looked around.

Ricky was standing in front of her, blocking her view of most of the crowd.

"Wassup Ricky?"

"Do you…need anything?"

"Dog's taking care of me, big guy," she reached a hand out to pat him on the shoulder but missed spectacularly. "He's on his way back."

"Would you like to sit down?" Ricky's voice had an irritating note of concern. "Perhaps in the VIP lounge?"

Helen perked up at the sound of that.

"There's a VIP lounge?"

"Yes, upstairs, would you like to follow me?"

"Um," she stood up straight, then promptly placed her hands back on the stage as she nearly fell over. "Oh fuck, uh yeah, yes."

"Can you walk?"

"I think so, why, you gonna carry me?"

"Would you like me to?" he answered as stone-faced as ever.

"M-maybe just next to me, arm on my shoulders kinda thing?"

"Of course," he moved next to her, providing steady support as she staggered toward the staircase.

It took twice as long as it should've, but before long they were up the staircase, then moving along the perimeter of the building towards a lounge filled with plush cushions, deep shadowy benches, and private tables.

"Would you like a private booth, or a public table?"

"Private, with a view of the dance floor. Can we do that?"

"Yes ma'am," he steered her towards the far end.

They landed at a booth which was surrounded on three sides by tall, freestanding panes of frosted glass. The fourth side faced the dance floor, and offered an excellent side view of Rylee as she worked. The semi-circular bench could probably fit six comfortably, and it was covered in a deep plush purple cushion. At the center of the setup was a black glass table that had a tall metal pole in the center of it that was anchored in the ceiling above.

"Thish is fun," Helen grabbed the pole and found that it spun freely.

Ricky said nothing, but directed Helen into her seat before placing himself next to the booth, hands clasped in front of him.

"Are you my babysitter now?"

"You are now my primary duty," he nodded. "My shift at the door is over, so I'm on DV duty."

"DV?"

"Distinguished visitor."

Sexy.

"Hey, how is Dog going to know–"

She was interrupted by the appearance of her waiter, he was carrying a new tray, one of the mirrored ones.

"Dog," she exclaimed with delight. "You found me!"

"Yes ma'am," he smiled as he sidled past Ricky. "Your powder and your drink, ma'am."

"You're worthless," she said in the same affectionate tone someone might use to say 'I love you.'

She lifted the glass and set it on the table, then turned her attention to the four neat lines of white powder on the mirror.

"Ah fuck, I don't have a straw," she fished around in her clutch for a dollar bill, but came up empty-handed. "Hey can you–"

Ricky was holding out a crisp hundred dollar bill.

"Thanks Ricky," she smiled, genuinely touched.

"My pleasure."

She rolled the bill and snorted the first line, pulling lightning directly into her veins.

"Whew," she dropped the bill and clapped her hands together. "Fuck that's good."

"Is there anything else I can provide?" Dog asked.

You need to take it easy.

You need to piss off.

Luciana-

Isn't here.

"Um," Helen's voice was over-loud as she tried to drown out the voices in her mind. "Dancers! I need a dancer, what's a pole without a dancer?"

"Do you have any *preferences* for your dancer, ma'am?"

"Surprise me."

Dog disappeared behind the panes of glass as Helen railed out another line and took a heavy drink of her martini. The coke pumped her heartrate up, her eyes felt too-wide, and she could feel a dryness in her mouth that the alcohol didn't quite get rid of.

"You think I'm a mess, huh?" she asked no one in particular.

No answer.

"Ricky," she turned a little too quickly, blurring all of reality until her eyes adjusted. "You think I'm a mess?"

"Not my place to say," he shrugged. "You're better behaved than some of the folks I've watched."

"But?"

"But you drink like someone trying to forget."

She nodded, laughing harshly and taking another drink.

"If that's what you want, you'll find it here."

"How the hell am I supposed to know what I want?" she mumbled.

Within minutes her dancers appeared.

One, a tall, slender black man in tight denim jeans and an open black vest, was currently riding the pole like a rodeo bronc. His abs had abs, and his body was a flowing, chiseled, statue of Adonis. The other was a petite asian woman with a winding dragon tattoo that curled around her body from her left ankle, up her hips, across her stomach, and then the full length of her right arm. She had short black hair cut at a harsh angle from the back of her head down to where it matched her jawline across her face, giving her a distinctly chic, runway look. She wore a lace bodysuit—blue, as Helen noted—and a pair of clear heels.

She'd forgotten their names almost immediately, but that hadn't stopped her from enjoying their company.

The man had been dancing on the table with the skill of a practiced athlete, resembling a human panther and exuding raw strength and sexuality. His movements suggested that he was a seasoned pro, and his pupils said he was flying nearly as high as she was.

The woman was more direct, whether as an invitation to Helen to participate or simply as her own preference, she'd been inching closer to Helen by the minute. Her small breasts were complimented by sloping sides and a firm, well muscled lower body. She was gorgeous; hell they both were, but despite the woman gyrating close enough to qualify as a lap dance, Helen couldn't focus.

You're just a pet.

A pet on a leash.

Shut up.

Go play in the yard, pet, go sit on your lead and play with your toys while the big kids talk.

All four lines of cocaine were gone, and a half dozen empty glasses occupied the space around her dancer's feet, but nothing was taking away the angst in her mind. She circled it, her thoughts chewing at her like a dog with a toy. Luciana had been gone how long? An hour? A week?

Would she even know unless someone *deigned* to tell her?

Why had she even left Tetiana's grove?

Because you didn't deserve to be there.

Because you have nothing of value to add.

She could feel the edges of her vision vibrating with every heartbeat, and the burn of alcohol and bile in her throat. It mixed with the scents of artificial cherry and old spice, of arousal, of sweat. and desperation.

"Do you know what this color means?" the woman in front of her drew her back to reality, erasing her scowl.

She was touching herself, with one hand cupping a breast and the other pressing hard against her barely contained sex.

"It means you can look *and* touch," she smiled, sliding the lace aside and revealing her perfectly smooth, soaking wet core.

Yes yes yes.

No.

Worried about your girlfriend?

Oh now you have issues with cheating? With the woman who left you to the wolves, threw you into a rave?

"I'm sorry," Helen stood, her own body throbbing in response to the woman.

She could feel her inner thighs soaked with more than sweat as she forced herself to stand shakily.

"I'm–"

But she shoved the woman aside, stumbling toward the entrance to the club. She was heedless of who she pushed, shoved, or bumped into on her path. She pressed on as the world started to collapse in around her. Her heart felt like it would explode and her stomach churned. Her throat felt like she'd swallowed acid and her vision was flickering in and out between reality and the quickly warping influence of her hallucinagenics.

Helen burst out the front door, startling a small cluster of people waiting to get in, and drawing the attention of both guards. They ignored her as she stumbled around the corner and into an alley, gulping air like a dying woman.

"Ma'am?"

She turned, steadying herself against the wall of the warehouse.

"Ricky?"

"I'm here," his words were calm, warm. "I'll stay with you."

His words triggered something inside of her and she immediately heaved, throwing up everything in her stomach into a dumpster and miraculously avoiding getting anything on her clothes.

Helen wasn't sure how long she was sick, but she threw up until nothing but thin yellow bile came out, and then dry-heaved after that.

"Come on," Ricky told her after a while.

He wrapped one of her arms over his shoulder, then lifted her bodily. Helen expected him to walk back to the front of the building, but instead he took her around back. The rear of the building had another door, but this one was centered in a well lit section of wall. The concrete was littered with cigarette butts and empty drink containers, and there were a couple of twenty-somethings in chef jackets smoking and laughing when they showed up.

Break room?

She'd been in enough service industry jobs in her life to recognize the smoke pit, and immediately she felt a little more at ease.

"Can you stand?"

"Yeah, I think so."

He set her down gingerly and she leaned against a steel railing, the world spinning and pulsing still. Empty stomach or not, she was still feeling the effects of the acid and Ricky seemed to glow with a dull gold, his eyes a curious icy blue and a little stormcloud swirling around his head.

"You worry a lot," Helen blurted out, pointing to the cloud.

"It's my job to worry."

"Do you like your job?"

"I love it, I found my purpose."

"Jesus," she laughed bitterly. "What's that feel like?"

"Feels…right, that's all."

They fell into a silence that lasted a few minutes until the two cooks left again.

"I'm sorry you're stuck with me," Helen admitted softly. "Probably for the best though."

"Why do you say that?"

"I'm a fuckin' mess, Ricky, and we ain't got time for that whole story."

"We've got *some* time," he pulled a pack of menthol cigarettes from his jacket and, after taking one, offered it to her.

She accepted, pulling a cigarette from the pack and allowing him to light it for her with an old fashioned flip lighter.

"I just," she took a long drag. "I wish I knew what I was doing. I feel…broken. Lost."

"Maybe you are."

"That's not very helpful," she bumped him with her shoulder.

"We're all broken in some way, and we all get lost," he blew a perfect smoke ring. "The key is to keep *moving*, keep pushing toward–"

"The light at the end of the tunnel?"

"If you wanna call it that," he shrugged.

"Yeah, with my luck it'd be an oncoming train."

"Look, sometimes life sucks. It hurts, it kicks you down, and it doesn't stop there," he nodded sagely, finished his cigarette then dropped the butt on the ground and dug it in with his shoe. "None of us make it out of life alive, but you can sure as hell fight 'til the bell."

Chapter Twelve

"You're pretty wise for a bouncer," she took another drag and stepped away, Ricky at her back. "Anyone ever tell you that?"

He didn't answer except to grunt, so she continued until she was close to the corner of the building.

"Oh now you're speechless?"

"Hrrk."

The noise was less grunt this time and more…*wet*.

"What was *that*?"

She turned and froze, the cigarette in her hand hanging limply from her fingers. Ricky was standing where he had been, though he'd turned in her direction as if to follow. But it wasn't the bouncer that paralyzed her with fear, it was the two skeletal claws protruding from his chest—and the *thing* they were attached to.

Whatever *it* was, it was mostly humanlike. It resembled nothing so much as a tall, impossibly gaunt human with black and blue mottled flesh. It was as though a man had been stretched to nearly eight feet tall and starved to death, with skin stretched across bone and cracked, shaggy lips overhanging sharp, blackened teeth.

Its face was the stuff of nightmares.

It had rotten, glassy eyes sunken far back into its skull, and its nose was gone, leaving a desiccated hole in the center of its skull. It was bald except for a few strands of greasy black hair that protruded from its scalp in blotchy patches. The thing's chin and neck were coated in crusty patches of dried, flaky red that Helen had a sinking feeling was old blood.

As she watched, it raised its face to the sky and let loose a horrid keening sound that pierced her eardrums like knives. She dropped to her knees, hands covering her ears automatically. The sound sent a shockwave of cold through her body, and she found herself shivering instantly, as though she were in the midst of a blizzard.

She couldn't move, and could only watch helplessly as the creature removed its claws from Ricky's back. The man—who only a moment ago had seemed so powerful, so untouchable, so *alive*—sank to the ground twitching and gurgling, blood flowing from his mouth.

With Ricky out of the way, she could see the creature in its entirety. Even hunched over, the emaciated being was massive. The arms were elongated out of proportion to the rest of it, which more or less stayed humanlike, and its knuckles grazed the ground as it stalked slowly forward. The hands, too, were over-large, and the first and second fingers were both nearly a foot long and each tipped with razor sharp claws instead of fingernails.

Helen tried to scream, tried to run, but she was rooted in place against her will.

The keening grew louder, and her ears screamed in protest. She could feel hot liquid dripping from her eardrums across her hands, but couldn't remove her hands to examine them closer. With every step, the chill in her body deepened, and by the time it was five feet away, she could no longer feel her hands or feet, nor her cheeks or nose.

The monster slowly raised a hand and Helen braced herself for the inevitable.

This isn't real. It can't be real.

You're gonna die.

No!

Finally.

When it struck, it did so with the speed of a cobra.

The hand lashed out across the space between them, claws pointed straight at Helen's chest, only to smash into a swirling barrier of greenish light mere inches from Helen's body.

Her wrist suddenly burned and she could see Tetiana's mark blazing brightly on her arm—and burning like the heating element of a stove.

The creature screeched again, then tried once more to attack her only to have its other hand bash against the barrier as well. Rage and frustration filled those hollow, lifeless eyes, and it battered against the shield over and over again, heedless of its own fingers breaking. She watched as its hands, mangled from smashing against her thin layer of protection, reassembled themselves with sickly crackling and crunching.

Seconds passed and the creature roared again, finally placing both hands against the barrier and squeezing. The too-sharp nails and claws sparked against Helen's protection, sending spiderwebs of darker green spinning across the swirling cascade of energy and finally, *finally*, breaking the spell of Helen's silence.

Her scream was high and piercing, not unlike the monster trying to kill her. She hardly even recognized the sound as coming from her own body. Her pulse pounded in her head and she could feel every muscle in her body straining to curl up as small as possible. She kept screaming until she was sure she'd pass out, but still the noise continued. Time seemed to stretch on forever with her eyes screwed tightly shut, but she couldn't get the gaunt, hungering face out of her mind.

She flinched as her body was hit with a spray of something cold and thick and wet, but her scream went on unabated.

"Helen!"

The voice was familiar.

"Helen, get up, Helen!"

Someone grabbed her shoulders and she lashed out instinctively, her foot connecting with someone or something resulting in a heavy 'oof.'

"Helen!"

Luciana!

She jerked her eyes open, scrambling backwards until she impacted the wall painfully.

Luciana was kneeling in front of where she'd been, one hand on her stomach and the other holding a five foot long *sword* covered in thick blackish liquid. The monstrosity was laying on the ground behind her in three pieces: the body split in two from shoulder to waist and the head sitting a few feet away.

Luciana was still wearing the slinky, strappy clubwear she'd arrived in. Her perfect razor sharp eyeliner and tan, toned body felt both completely natural in the presence of a bloodied sword, and at the same time was a jarring juxtaposition that further derailed Helen's brain.

"Helen," Luciana glanced left and right down the alley, then turned back to her. "Helen, we have to go *right now.*"

"Wha-whatthefuckwasthat," Helen sobbed, tears suddenly pouring down her face.

A sizzling sound had her crawling backward and pressing herself back against the wall as though she could get through the barrier if she just tried hard enough.

She looked at the pieces of the monster, which were now sizzling and bubbling away into a dark smoke and drifting up into the air. An acrid odor assaulted her nose and she held her breath as the creature dissolved completely, leaving no trace behind.

"L-l-luciana," she stammered past chattering teeth. "Is this real, are you real?"

"Yes," the woman stood and took a slow step forward.

"I'm so cold," Helen blurted out, her whole body shivering. "Is it cold out?"

"It's a side effect of the Wendigo," Luciana's voice was calm. "It will pass in time, but time isn't something we have right now."

"Wendigo? Time?"

Helen's mind was a fractured mirror. Safety, security, hell *reality* was a warm summer's day and she was standing in cold October rain.

"Baby, you need to come with me," Luciana held out a hand. "Tetiana's got the car up front, but we have to get out of here before more show up."

More?

"More!?"

Helen felt faint, she wavered on her feet as the world around her switched rapidly between black and white, normal, and swirling technicolor. She tried to stand but wound up back on her ass on the cold concrete, the world spinning until it finally faded to black.

The last thing she saw was Luciana kneeling down in front of her.

She woke up some time later, wind whipping past her face and dislodging her carefully prepared hair. Even before she opened her eyes, she became aware of her cold, sweat-slick body, and the horrid taste of stale vomit and alcohol in her dry mouth. She opened her eyes blearily, recognizing only blurred lights and the strangely quiet inside of the sportscar she was riding in.

Luciana was driving and—judging from the muted color changes and amorphous edges of the woman's body—she was still under the influence. She tried to lift her head from the headrest and found her whole body was bone tired. Her muscles barely responded at all. As her senses turned back online, she noted a stinging burning pain in her hands, toes, nose and cheeks.

"Ow," she mumbled, looking down at her pink hands. The tips of her fingers were pale by comparison, and had significantly less pain—and feeling. "What's wrong with me?"

"Frostbite."

Luciana's response was clipped, and her words were accompanied by smooth but sharp turns as they wove in and out of traffic.

Whether it was the drugs, the alcohol, or her encounter with the wendigo, Helen couldn't seem to get the city to come into focus. The buildings, traffic, and even the people they were passing, were just a distorted blur of color outside of the relative stability of the vehicle.

As the wendigo returned to her mind, Helen's pulse skyrocketed. Her body flooded with what little adrenaline she had left and she jerked upright fast enough to lock the seatbelt.

"Slow down," Luciana tried and failed to give her a reassuring smile. "You're going to feel weakened from the club and–"

"The fucking *monster*?"

"Yes."

By the time they'd reached the hotel, Helen was aware enough to think a little straighter, but Luciana was more close-lipped than Helen had experienced yet. For her own part, Helen was stuck in a loop, replaying the horror of the alleyway and slipping further and further from the here and now.

She allowed herself to be tugged from the vehicle and brought inside, but she perceived nothing of the lobby, the elevator, or their two attachees from before. The next thing she knew, she was standing, shivering in the middle of the main room of the suite, her arms hanging limply at her side and her eyes unfocused.

"Helen," Luciana stepped in front of her and gently took hold of her shoulders. "We need to sober you up, and more importantly we need to *warm* you up."

She nodded dumbly, not really hearing the woman's words.

"I'm going to take you to the shower, ok?"

Luciana took her non-response as an affirmative and steered her to the bathroom before turning on the shower and then helping her out of her outfit.

"You pop in here," she gently maneuvered her into the stream of warm water. "I need to get our things ready to go."

"Go?"

Her mumbled question went unanswered as Luciana disappeared into the rest of the suite.

The warmth from the water *hurt* her hands, face, and feet. The rest of her body was grateful for the warmth, the steady pressure, and the cleansing effect. She watched with detached horror as the blackish blood from the wendigo stained the floor of the shower before spiraling into the drain below.

All black, no red.

She thought of Ricky. The horror on his face, the surprise, the pain in his eyes.

He died because of you.

Because he dared to be kind to you.

Be near you.

She couldn't even make herself argue.

The man's death pressed down on her until she found herself sitting instead of standing, then finally laying on the floor of the shower in the fetal position. She squeezed her hands tight, wishing the burn of her frostbite would wipe her mind clean.

But it didn't.

Tears mixed with the water as she broke, her body unable to hold back the horror. She shook harder than she ever had. No cold, no drug, nothing had ever made her body quake and tremble the way it did now. It was like her body wasn't her own, like the worst of her dissociative episode without the detachment, without the numbness she craved.

"Helen?"

When she didn't respond, Luciana entered the room and took stock of her, though Helen didn't raise her eyes to meet her gaze.

"Oh baby, I'm so sorry," the woman murmured, climbing into the shower and sitting down beside her, heedless of her clothing, her makeup, or anything else. "I'm so sorry."

Luciana lifted her, wrapping Helen in her arms, and cradling her like a baby with her head against the larger woman's shoulder. Helen clung to her like a drowning man to a piece of flotsam.

"This should never have happened," Luciana stroked her hair as it lay wet against her back and shoulders. "I should never have left you alone."

Hele gripped her tighter, grateful for her lover's powerful build.

"The wendigo…I'm not sure how it found us so quickly. I didn't expect it and I should have," blame permeated Luciana's voice. "But it's gone now, it can't hurt you."

"B-b-but," Helen's breath was shaking and her teeth chattered. "You said there were more?"

"There are," Luciana agreed grimly. "Which is why we need to leave. How are your hands?"

"Cold."

"But you can feel them?"

Helen nodded, flexing her extremities painfully.

"Good, then I don't need to use magic to avoid any permanent damage. That'll help us get off of his radar."

"The Smiling Man?"

Luciana nodded.

"I promise you, Helen, I'll answer your questions once we're out of here, ok? We just need to get moving. We need distance."

"Ok."

"Tetiana's going to cover our tracks as best she can," Luciana continued. "But that'll only last so long."

Another nod.

"I set out some clothes for you on the bed. I just need to get this blood off."

"Ricky," Helen looked up finally. "Is he?"

"Ricky?"

"The bouncer."

Luciana's silence was answer enough.

A few minutes later, Helen was pulling on a pair of shorts next to their bed, which just a few hours ago had seemed so warm, so inviting, so safe.

"What was that thing?"

"A wendigo," Luciana tossed a balled up shirt to Helen, who caught it. "Someone corrupted by dark magic."

"That was a *person*?"

"At some point, yes," she nodded. "Someone who made a deal with a Fae in exchange for power and finally paid the price."

"Jesus," Helen yanked on her sneakers.

"Humans weren't meant to hold magic," Luciana explained, waiting at the door. "Some humans bargain for it, but it creates a hunger in them that can never be sated. Eventually, they are nothing more than cold and pain and starvation, begging for scraps of magic from their masters."

Helen followed her to the elevator. When the doors opened, they found Lily within.

"Your car is waiting for you, ladies."

"Thank you."

Helen stifled her questions during the awkward, too-slow ride to the lobby, but the second they were far enough across the foyer, she started in again.

"How did it find us?"

"They must've been tracking us since we left the manor," Luciana frowned. "With the wendigo dead–"

"It is, right? Dead?"

"Yes, it's dead."

"But there could be more," Helen surmised.

"Yes. We have to hope he only sent one, and get out while we can."

The noisy city air was no longer exciting. Now, every sound screamed danger, and every light and passing car set Helen further on edge.

She took a deep, grounding breath, and allowed herself to retreat within the safety of dissociation. Her shrinks had always told her, over the years, that dissociation was a dangerous and maladaptive coping mechanism; that she *shouldn't* actively encourage the response, that it would only exacerbate her problems.

Bullshit.

Helen walked backwards out of her own body and mind, detaching until she was as much a passenger as a driver.

"Come on," Luciana held the door open for Helen to climb in, then hopped in the driver's seat.

Even putting distance between herself and reality, she didn't breathe easily until they were far outside the city several hours later. Even then, her eyes were glued to the landscape around them, imagined shapes and shadows lurking everywhere.

"I'm sorry, Helen, I never should've gotten complacent."

Helen nodded absentmindedly, but said nothing.

"The wendigo's energy will be returning to The Smiling Man," she explained despite the flat, glassy stare of her passenger. "They aren't true Fae, just power hungry vessels."

A silence fell that seemed to indicate she was waiting for a response, so Helen reverted to an old habit she'd picked up after being asked 'how does that make you feel' one too many times.

"How do they gain their power, exactly?" she asked, not really listening to the answer.

"Drinking Fae blood as part of a dark ritual."

"Mhmm," Helen nodded.

"It grants them powers but enslaves them—Helen, are you listening?"

"Sorry, yeah," she lied. "Why, um, why did it make me so cold?"

"Legend says the first wendigos were cannibals, people who were forced to do horrific things during blizzards or long winter famines," Luciana shrugged. "Most likely the desperate bastards turned to the Fae for help and got more than they bargained for, then paid the price. Over centuries, my kind perfected the ritual, made it more advantageous to the Fae."

"So, do many Fae make these…*things*?"

"No," Luciana answered firmly. "It is deeply frowned upon, many of us consider it a perversion."

Her words faded into silence and Helen was more than happy to continue detaching from herself. Rather than face the uncomfortable realities of her present situation.

Luciana was less willing to let the conversation die.

"Helen?"

“Hmm?”

“I’m…worried, about you.”

She doesn’t trust you.

She knows you’re weak.

“Why?” she responded cagily.

“Helen, you watched someone *die*, that’s–”

“Luciana,” Helen turned away. “It’s fine.”

“Helen, that's serious trauma,” Luciana pressed. “You can’t just shove that down and not deal with it.”

“Yes I can,” Helen pushed back firmly.

“It’s not healthy–”

“It’s *safe*,” Helen snapped. “Luciana, I don’t want to talk about this right now.”

Silence.

“Please?”

Helen couldn’t help the raw emotion that slipped into her final, pleading word.

“Alright,” Luciana sighed. “Alright, fine, but I don’t want to just sit here in silence.”

Helen chewed her lip, torn between letting the woman in and maintaining her distance as she had always done. On the one hand, Luciana had broken through most of her defense in just a matter of days. On the other, they'd hardly known each other for a few weeks—and part of that time, she'd been in a magic induced coma.

"Penny for your thoughts?"

"What did you talk to Tetiana about."

It was a statement, not a question, and honestly, Helen expected a vague answer, or perhaps even to be blown off entirely.

"I needed to know some of what has changed since I was last out and about," she answered plainly. "The Fae world is a vicious, ever-changing landscape of power and balance. As an oracle, Tetiana has a unique level of neutrality and therefore, safety—and she's also much closer with the elders than most of us."

"She's close with the elders?"

"Yes, the elders carefully guard and...*guide* the oracles as best they can. Partly for the sake of the balance in the Fae community, and partly for–"

"Power?"

"Yes."

"So what did you find out?"

Despite her best efforts, Luciana's conversation was pulling her back from the distant place she'd allowed her mind to wander. Her interest was too great and the importance of their talk was too real for her to ignore it.

"The Smiling Man is after me," she visibly tightened her grip on the steering wheel, her jaw set. "He's still mad I made him bleed, I suppose. Not that he was ever the forgiving type."

"Aren't there other dragon hunters out there?"

"We're a rare breed, and it's a lethal profession."

"So no one is brave enough, that's what you're saying."

Luciana sighed again, heavier this time.

"Yes," she nodded curtly. "He's grown powerful enough that some of the elders are worried he'll make a play for one of them, and no hunter will touch him. A half dozen have tried since my seclusion and all of them were consumed,"

"So what do we do?"

"I can't ignore this any more," Luciana's voice dropped low. "I created this problem, it's time for me to fix it."

"Ok, how do we fix it?"

"That's just it," Luciana ran her fingers through her hair. "I can't drag you into a fight like this."

"Luciana," Helen's voice cracked. "I'm already in it!"

"I know, and I'll never forgive myself for that," Luciana glanced over at her. "But I don't have anywhere to take you either, so…"

"So the safest place *would* be with you, wouldn't it?"

She wants out.

Of course she does.

Do fire stations take abandoned adults too, or just babies?

"Unfortunately."

Unfortunately?

"So what do we do now?"

"We go visit one of the elders, and hope they're willing to intervene."

Chapter Thirteen

Six hours later, the two women were back in the mountains.

Their plan had been to avoid major highways, hopefully keeping themselves further under the radar of The Smiling Man. The couple had started out on highway 80 until they hit Sacramento, then jumped on 50 eastbound and up into the mountains. The weather had been pleasant starting out, but now bad luck or bad timing had them in the middle of an early season storm. Visibility had tanked and snow was coming down sideways, and Helen's modified car was already struggling on turns and climbs. Around an hour ago, they'd fallen into place behind a big rig that was going forty-five in a seventy, but it looked like he was finally taking an exit that they weren't.

"Luciana," Helen gripped the 'oh shit handle' above her window for the umpteenth time. "Are you good to drive in this?"

"Is anyone?" Luciana grumbled, squinting through the blizzard surrounding them.

"Maybe we should pull off, get a hotel or something–ohshitfuck!"

She scrunched her eyes shut as they fishtailed at the bottom of a steep decline, not breathing until Luciana straightened the car out.

"We're on a time crunch," Luciana looked over at her, worry written in the lines of her face. "But, maybe you're right. Maybe we need to let this storm ride itself out."

Helen tried to respond, but her stomach was in knots and she worried that if she opened her mouth she'd throw up.

Add car trauma to the list.

True to her word, Luciana took the next exit. They couldn't see what was written on the sign, but it was a gamble they had to take.

The exit ramp opened to a roundabout and they picked a direction at random. None of the roads were plowed and layers of ice and snow conspired to pull the vehicle off the road, or at least to a stop.

"What the hell is this?" Luciana frowned as they found themselves entering a large empty parking lot.

"A rest stop maybe?"

But there were no buildings visible, just a flat asphalt space big enough for perhaps thirty vehicles, and a sign at the far end. The space was ringed in pine trees, all heavy with fresh fallen snow, and on one side it looked out over a cliff and what certainly would be a stunning vista on a day with better weather.

"Let's check the sign," Helen prompted, worried if they stopped moving the car would truly be stuck.

They crunched across the frozen waste to the sign, which was on the leeward side of a large tree and was still miraculously clear enough of snow that it could be read.

They got closer and were able to see two things: The first, a sign that indicated they were at the 'Red Lake Parking Area,' and the second being an almost entirely buried firewatch tower.

"Do you suppose anyone is in there?" Helen asked as they ground to a halt.

"I don't know, do we want to find out?"

Helen thought about it a moment, her anxiety about the drive warring with her fear that somehow The Smiling Man would be waiting for them.

"No, let's keep going."

"Helen–"

"I'm sure, I don't want to meet some stranger and have it go wrong."

"Alright," Luciana hit the gas lightly and both women frowned as their wheels spun in the snow.

"Fuck."

She gave it more gas, but the car didn't move an inch no matter how hard the tires squealed. They were door-deep in fast falling snow and the sedan didn't have a prayer of getting itself out any time soon.

Unless they used magic?

"Should we, uh," Helen wiggled her fingers and jerked her head toward the window. "Help ourselves out?"

"I…" Luciana hesitated. "I could, but if there are more wendigo on our tail, it'll light up like a beacon and I couldn't outrun them in this, not a chance.

"Ok, plan b," Helen sighed. "I guess we go knock on the door."

Luciana half smiled and shrugged helplessly.

"You want to do the honors?"

Helen sighed back, but nodded.

A few minutes later she was wrapped in her warmest clothes and had her backpack in her lap—no point in making two trips after all.

"Ok, here we go!"

She pushed open the door, which took a bit of effort given the snow was now several inches above the bottom of the door.

Immediately, she was hit by a blast of cold air and wet snow.

Mother fucker God damnit fuck shit.

She and Luciana trudged through the winter wasteland, every step a struggle as they worked their way toward the stairs of the fire watch tower. The snow was heavy and wet, not the light powder that Helen was used to in Tennessee, and it was in quantities that, to her, looked absolutely apocalyptic. This was the kind of thing she saw on the news or in a movie—not in real life. They started out side by side, but by the time they hit the bottom of the stairs, Luciana was leading, her strong thighs plowing through the snow and ice with relative ease, and Helen was trailing behind her and taking advantage of the path she'd cleared.

"Be careful on the ice," Luciana glanced back at her. "The stairs are really slick."

True to her girlfriend's word, Helen's foot slipped an inch or so as soon as she put weight on the first step. She braced herself and—against her own desire to stay warm—reached her ungloved hand out to the ice-clad railing.

The bite of the cold metal drained the feeling from her fingers in seconds, and by the time they reached the door at the top of the third flight of stairs, her fingers were as numb as her face.

The two shared another look before Luciana raised her fist and banged firmly on the tightly shuttered wooden door. The sound was nearly lost in the howling wind, but certainly anyone within would have heard them.

Right?

A minute passed with no answer, despite Luciana knocking twice more.

"We're gonna freeze to death out here," Helen yelled over the worsening storm, her eyes stinging from the cold.

"Hold on," Luciana frowned, taking a half step back.

Helen made room, expecting her to look in one of the frost-covered windows, but Luciana had a different idea.

The woman leaned forward, dropped a shoulder, and slammed into the door with enough force to rattle the windows and shake some snow loose from the eaves of the roof. Icicles clattered to the ground and landed in the snow as the door burst open, and Luciana stumbled into the room.

Helen jumped, taken off guard, but then quickly followed.

"Well, safe to say no one is home," Luciana smiled as she forced the door shut behind Helen.

The tower was exceedingly simple in its layout—essentially a single-room cabin with a small bathroom behind the only door. The walls were half-length windows all the way around, though all of the glass was covered by heavy storm shutters at the moment. The interior was all bare wood and warm tones, right down to the orange enamel coating on the decades-old kitchen appliances and the rust-colored bedspread on the queen size in the corner.

There was a pantry of sorts: wire racks filled with canned and dry goods and about a million different sized canisters of different spices. This was, of course, against one part of the wall in the kitchen area, which had a gas stove connected by a blue hose to a propane tank.

A big, black iron woodburning stove dominated another corner of the space, its shiny metal stovepipe disappearing above the rafters and through the roof, and beside it was a sizable amount of dry, neatly stacked firewood.

"I'm guessing that's our heat," Helen rubbed her upper arms, willing the motion to heat her cold body. "I'll get a fire going."

"I'll check the kitchen, see if we have the stuff to make dinner."

Helen nodded, then walked over to the woodburning stove. A few boxes of matches and some small pine tapers were set atop one side of the woodpile, so she grabbed both as well as a couple of small hunks of wood. The stove was well maintained and well oiled, and the combustion chamber had been recently cleaned, so it took her all of five minutes to arrange a neat little stack of wood and shavings.

The pine taper she held took a flame easily from one of the matches, and the well-seasoned wood caught fire just as rapidly. Within moments a small but growing fire was heating the cold metal and working its way toward warming the room.

"Pretty good," Luciana teased. "I figured woodburners had gone out of style."

"They have, old lady," Helen laughed. "But thankfully my grammy still has one."

"Southern Charm?"

"You know't," Helen lathered on her native accent *thick*. "Nun them city folk 'member the old ways, but we do."

"Well I'm glad," Luciana's smile faltered a moment as she shot a wistful look back at the kitchen. "Because the propane tank is empty, so anything we're cooking is gonna be old school."

"Oh that's no problem," Helen smiled, heading into the kitchen.

She collected some powdered chicken bouillon, some dried sage and basil, a bit of rosemary, and half a dozen other spices, a box of orzo, a few cans of vegetables, and some canned chicken, as well as a cast iron dutch oven and a worn wooden spoon.

"Chicken soup ok?"

"Sure," Luciana smiled, stripping out of her snowy clothes and watching Helen with curious intent.

Helen set her ingredients down next to the stove, then popped outside to cram the dutch oven full of snow. She returned a moment later, shaking snow out of her hair, and set the pot on top of the woodburning stove, where it immediately sizzled to life.

It was the work of just a few more minutes to open the cans and throw all of her ingredients into the rapidly melting snow, and when she was done and had given it a stir, she set the lid on with a smile.

"There ya go, soup's on," she turned around, hands on her hips. "That's one thing solv…"

Helen trailed off, her mind grinding to a halt as she drank in the sight of Luciana on the bed. She was wearing a flattering black bra, and a matching set of underwear that highlighted her hips and thighs. The woman was propped up on one elbow as she lay on her side reading a book, her hair in a still-wet mess and her feet stretched out in the general direction of the stove.

"Hmm," she looked up, her brow furrowed from concentrating.

"God you're gorgeous," Helen sighed.

Luciana smiled broadly, though her cheeks flushed a bit.

"You could join me," she patted the bedspread.

Helen headed toward the bed but Luciana held up a hand with a frown.

"You're not planning on wearing wet, *cold* clothes into our bed," she narrowed her eyes.

"Hmm," Helen kicked out of her sneakers and looked down at herself.

For the most part her outer layer was more damp than truly wet, her hair most of all. She considered obliging, but chose to listen to her lesser angels instead.

"You'll warm me up, won't you," she looked up innocently, taking a big step toward the bed.

"Helen," Luciana scooted back a foot. "Helen, you wouldn't dare–Ahh!"

Helen leapt into the bed, wrapping her protesting girlfriend in a damp, chilly hug.

"Helen," Luciana was laughing as she pried the smaller woman off of her. "Helen, you *fiend*."

They tussled on the bed a moment, and when they came to a breathless stop, Helen was laying with her back on the bed and Luciana was propped up over her, holding herself aloft with both arms

"Let me help you," Luciana said softly, effortlessly holding herself up with one hand and unbuttoning Helen's shirt with the other.

Helen felt a rush of warmth in her face as Luciana's fingers lingered on every button. She allowed the woman to undress her slowly, methodically. Every garment that she shed left her skin cooler and her chest tighter, her pulse quicker.

"You're beautiful," Luciana murmured, pulling off Helen's pants and tossing them carelessly beside the bed.

She ran a strong, warm hand, her fingers splayed, up Helen's calf, then thigh. Her palm left a trail of blazing heat as it crossed the band of her panties and continued its journey up her side and across her shoulder blade before tucking Helen's hair out of her face.

Helen's breath caught, and she felt a familiar pressure growing within her. It was arousal, yes, but her attraction was a thin veil over the turbulent currents of unprocessed trauma and grief—things she wasn't ready to face yet.

"Your eyes are so stormy."

"They are?" Helen blinked in surprise

Luciana nodded, cupping the side of her face. The woman's own dark eyes were filled with obvious concern, faint wrinkles in her brow.

"Hey, um, Helen? Listen–"

Helen raised her head off the bed and locked lips with the woman, cutting her off mid sentence with a kiss so laden with desperation that Luciana couldn't possibly misinterpret it.

"Baby--"

Helen ignored her, wrapping her arms around the woman's shoulders and pulling her close before rolling her over. Now astride her lover, she broke the kiss long enough to fling her hair over her shoulder and then re-engaged the woman. Luciana's body responded in kind, her strong hands finding Helen's hips and holding her in place even as Helen started to rock, grinding herself against Luciana.

She could feel her sex soaking the utilitarian blue panties she wore, and her nipples were prominent as they struggled against the thin fabric of her bra. The fabric and their skin rubbed together smoothly, the smooth fabric of their underwear gliding soundlessly as both of the women's breathing became less steady.

"May I?" Luciana breathed, as one hand snuck up and paused at the clasp on Helen's bra.

Helen nodded wordlessly and gasped a little as Luciana flicked her fingers and set the bra falling down her arms. It took the work of a few seconds to extricate herself, and in that time Luciana took her own bra off, leaving Helen with a loopy grin as her full bust came into view.

Helen slipped a hand down between them, her fingers sliding into place between their vulvas so that as she rocked, it rubbed against both Luciana's clitoris and her own.

Luciana moaned, her hips tipping upward to place more pressure on Helen's fingers.

The woman was wet and ready, her lips puffy with desire and a heat that turned Helen on even more.

"Fuck I love your fingers," Luciana groaned.

Helen smiled as she scooted back, affording herself a better angle, and hooked her fingers under the edge of Luciana's underwear.

"These fingers?"

"Mhmm," Luciana's eyes sparkled.

Helen pulled the fabric to the side, drinking in the sight of the woman before dipping first one, and then two fingers inside. Luciana's muscles rippled around her fingers, her pussy squeezing tightly under Helen's careful attention.

"I want to taste you," Helen admitted, licking her lips in anticipation.

"Yes please," Luciana bucked a little at the thought. "But only if I get the same treat."

Helen flushed with heat as they locked eyes. Luciana lifted a finger and spun it in the air, indicating that Helen should turn.

"Come here."

Helen stripped out of her underwear before turning, positioning her vulva directly above Luciana's face.

She'd seen sixty-nining in porn, obviously, but she'd never actually done it before in real life—not that she'd admit it. She jumped as Luciana's hands snaked up her thighs and took firm handfuls of her ass. Hopefully she liked the view?

Helen felt unexpectedly *vulnerable*. She was bared to her lover in all her glory, her thighs lightly touching Luciana's cheeks. She bit her lip, knowing that Luciana couldn't see the red in her cheeks but that she could certainly see Helen's arousal. What was she supposed to do, obviously she couldn't just like—was she supposed to go down or was Luciana supposed to come up?

"Let's get these off," Helen announced as sexily as possible, trying to fight back her self-consciousness.

She stretched forward as she pulled her lover's panties down, and in so doing she brought her sex close enough for Luciana to dart her face forward and bury her tongue between Helen's legs.

She squealed with pleasure as the woman's tongue parted her lips, curled around her clit, and then plunged within her.

That answers that.

"F-f-fuck," she struggled to hold herself up well enough to crawl back to Luciana's waiting folds. She placed a hand on either of Luciana's thighs and tried to catch her breath. Luciana was as passionate as she was talented, and Helen could feel her firm, warm tongue exploring every inch of her lips, her clitoris, and within.

She took another longing-filled look at Luciana's core, her hips already shaking from the passionate, *energetic*, attention she was receiving, then brought her own mouth down to Luciana's pussy.

Her taste was delicate, with a sharpness that Helen relished every time she ate a girl out. Helen could taste her arousal, her lips and chin instantly slick. She could feel Luciana's lips trembling, could feel her canal squeezing her tongue as she twisted and turned it, her movements slow, methodical, and rhythmic.

Luciana's tongue ran a circle around her clit and Helen responded in kind, relishing the shiver that ran through the woman's body as she circled the tiny button of pleasure with increasing pressure and frequency.

The women were both drawing ragged breaths within minutes as they raced toward a shared climax.

Helen came first, her whole body rolling as Luciana brought wave after wave of pleasure coursing through her—her clit throbbed with every stroke of the woman's tongue, her ass cheeks hurt from how hard Luciana squeezed, and her thighs were sore from how hard her muscles were trembling.

Stars popped in front of her as she squirmed, unable to escape Luciana's hungry mouth while the woman's hands were firmly clamping down on her hips and ass.

As soon as she could do more than cry out and shake, Helen redoubled her own efforts. Within moments, Luciana was writhing beneath her, her hands clawing at the bedsheets and her hips shaking.

When the fireworks ended, Helen righted herself, cuddling up next to Luciana as the pair caught their breaths.

"Not bad for a girl with no magic?"

"Felt like magic to me," Luciana laughed before yawning widely. "Certainly enough to wear me out."

Helen found herself surprisingly tired as well. Now that the sexual tension and energy had been drained and the stress of the last few days was catching up, she felt like she could sleep for a week.

Luciana's heartbeat conspired to lull her to sleep as well, her steadying, slowing breaths a lullaby that couldn't be ignored.

"I think I might love you," Helen mumbled, laying her head on Luciana's shoulder and allowing the woman to wrap an arm around her.

A heartbeat passed before Helen realized what she'd just said, but the second she did she froze as stiff as a board.

Did you just drop the L word you fucking lunatic?

"I think I love you, too," Luciana muttered, her fingers tracing tiny points of heat against Helen's skin.

Helen raised her head, eyes wide, and prepared to further the conversation, but Luciana was already snoring softly.

Helen half-smiled, then gently pulled the comforter off the bed before draping it over the sleeping woman.

Maybe she'll forget you said it.

Helen stood, crept quietly over to the soup, and gave it a stir while her lips broke into a smile so wide it hurt her blazing cheeks.

She said it back though.

Chapter Fourteen

Helen glanced over at the bed.

Luciana had been asleep for nearly an hour and in that time she'd managed to roll herself into a burrito of blankets, one bare leg striking out and a thin line of drool running down her perfect cheek onto the pillow. Helen couldn't help but marvel that even in the less-than-graceful state of slumber, she was *beautiful.*

The soup was done, it had been for a while and was now set off to the side just close enough to the stove to stay warm. Meanwhile, Helen was enjoying a steaming mug of instant coffee and wandering around the small space, her legs as restless as her mind.

Why did you say that?

We meant it, didn't we?

She said it back.

Did she? You probably made that up.

"Stop," she rubbed the bridge of her nose. "She said it, she did."

But there was nowhere in the small space to run away from her thoughts.

Desperate for distraction, she walked to the nearest window. The storm was still raging on, though the sky had darkened a bit. Thick snow flurried past and frost touched the edges of the glass, despite the considerable warmth given off by their woodburning stove.

They had plenty of food, water, and firewood for an extended stay—a thought that Helen minded less than she ought to—and the building seemed absolutely secure against the brutal winter storm.

Helen found herself daydreaming that the pair would have to stay a few days—a steamy romance in the snow fit for a harlequin romance novel.

Long enough to be found.

Long enough to be killed.

She shivered at the thought, goosebumps prickling her skin.

She'd put on a loose fitting t-shirt from her bag, but was still wandering around pantless. Despite her clothing and the stove, a chill ran up her spine as she considered the horrible cold and fear she'd felt in the presence of the wendigo.

What else lurked out there, waiting to pounce? What dangers lay in the future, and why hadn't she asked Tetiana to tell her her future.

Because you're afraid you don't have one.

Helen zeroed in on the feeling of helplessness she'd felt, the desperate inability to do *anything* to the wendigo. If it hadn't been for Tetiana's charm and Luciana's…*badassery*, she'd be dead.

She wasn't an overly physical kid growing up, and she didn't have the fanatical, gun-worshiping tendencies of many of her neighbors, but she had grown up a Tennessean and was more than comfortable with a firearm.

Unfortunately, she'd made the executive decision a few years ago that a gun might not be the safest thing for her to own.

She was regretting that now, wishing she'd followed her mother's advice and kept a 'just in case' revolver or something.

Actually, could wendigo even be killed with a bullet? Did it *have* to be a giant silver sword?

If you asked questions, you'd probably know some of these answers, idiot.

Her thoughts hounded her, denying her the rest and peace she craved as she sat quietly watching the snow pile up around them. She lost track of time, measuring instead by the number of cups of coffee she drank. She was midway through her third when she heard Luciana stirring behind her.

"What time is it?"

Luciana's words were muffled, the kind of leaden, sleepy voice you'd expect from a college freshman missing her first class after a party.

"Time to get up, sleepyhead," Helen sang back.

"Alright, alright," Luciana yawned, stretching wide. "God that smells amazing."

"Help yourself."

Helen watched her over the top of her mug, enjoying the lithe, naked form of her lover as she slipped out of bed and over to the soup where Helen had left a bowl and spoon for her.

"Hey can we, er, talk?"

"Of course," Luciana laughed as she secured a bowl of soup and stepped over to Helen.

She took a seat beside the combination counter-table and looked at Helen expectantly.

Well?

Helen smiled back, but the words she needed to form a coherent sentence were evading her.

Say something you fucking weirdo.

"So wendigo," she managed at last.

"Mhmm," Luciana sipped the flavorful broth, a contented smile on her face.

"Do you have to kill them with a sword or, I guess how does that work and *why* do you have a giant ass sword?"

Luciana laughed harder than Helen expected.

"Ok so wendigo can only be killed by silver or iron, thus the sword," Luciana held her hand out and the sword blinked into existence, its dark, leather-wrapped handle resting firmly in her hand. "Thus the *silver-plated* sword."

"Couldn't you just use a gun?"

"You could," Luciana shrugged. "But they're very durable and most bullets don't have iron in them, they have lead."

Obviously.

"Right," Helen grimaced in embarrassment. "So you use the sword because…?"

"Old habit," Luciana shrugged. "Most of us dragon hunters picked a weapon and stuck with it over the centuries, modifying it and customizing it over the years. We try to craft something that is…multipurpose."

"Meaning it can kill lots of stuff?"

"Yes, a well built hunting weapon is a very carefully crafted and irreplaceable item. We guard them jealously."

"So is that why you had to give away Askarii's spear?"

Luciana stiffened, then set down her spoon.

"Yes," she said with obvious difficulty. "Askarii's spear had something of a reputation. Even I don't know what all it was composed of—it is taboo to ask too much about another hunter's weapon—and for a time it was believed it could kill anything."

"Could it?"

"I used to think so," Luciana's shoulders drooped. "But no, not anything."

"The Smiling Man?"

"Yes, neither my sword nor her spear wounded him, and she paid the price."

Luciana ate in silence as Helen digested the information. Several minutes passed before Helen interrupted the quiet with more questions.

"What brought you to America?"

Luciana lifted her eyes and met Helen's curious gaze.

"A dragon, actually," she replied. "The first I ever took on by myself."

"You followed a dragon across the *ocean* to hunt it?"

"It was 1539, and the dragon was masquerading as a conqueror, which wasn't particularly unique at the time," she answered. "He was called Hernando De Soto, a conquistador from the area in Spain where I was living."

"What happened?"

"Well, by then he was already famous for butchering the Inca, and he was headed to the New World to 'pacify' it," she shook her head softly. "I had parted ways with Arlen already and cut my teeth on lesser skirmishes, but something in the way De Soto spoke about the natives in the New World boiled my blood. I followed him across the sea and hunted him down. I met many of the native nations, helped them deal with supernatural threats, and learned their ways. It took me three years to corner De Soto, but I got him. His back was to the Mississippi River, and he was low on men and supplies, so I helped lead a raid with a group of Ojibwe braves. We lost several good men and women, but I made sure his heart stopped by the close of day. Officially, I think his cause of death was 'disease,' but the cowards buried his body in the river so that the natives would still fear him."

"Holy shit," Helen was nearly speechless. "So then, why did you stay? Why not go back to Spain?"

"To tell you the truth, I fell in love with the people here. With the land. The First Nations lived so much more closely with the natural world than Europeans did. They embraced the land for what it was rather than try to cut, dig, chop, and burn it until it bent to their will. There weren't many Fae over here at first, and being one of the first few, I was able to travel freely and use my magic to help, to guide, and to protect."

"Did other dragons come?"

"Many," Luciana nodded. "The lure of a new land was a tempting thing—imagine the riches, the power, and the isolation to be found. That's how I really got to know Askarii, actually. She was traveling with the Sioux in the Northern Great Plains at the time…"

Luciana's soup sat forgotten as her eyes glazed over. Helen recognized the look, it was one she frequently wore when dissociating or dwelling in her thoughts and memories.

"Askarii and I, we garnered quite a reputation. We were this land's defenders, dragon hunters known far and wide."

Lucinna scoffed.

"We were founding members of the Praetorian Club, helped shape the next generation of hunters, we thought we were invincible."

A pause.

"We were wrong."

Helen sipped her coffee, waiting politely for her girlfriend to continue, if she chose to.

"We faced down The Smiling Man as he was posing as a military officer, an advisor to Andrew Jackson–"

"The *President?*"

"He wasn't the president then," Luciana frowned. "Just another officer hell bent on slaughtering the 'savages' who already inhabited this country. He decimated the Creek nation, and they called him 'hero.'"

"Wait so *he* wasn't the dragon, the dragon was an advisor to him?"

"Yes," Luciana stood and stepped away, her back—along with those visible scars—to Helen. "We'd never encountered one like him before. He was content to sit in the shadows, to wait, to whisper poison into the ears of those he could manipulate. We'd never met a dragon clever enough, or with enough restraint, to rule from behind the throne."

"So what did you do?"

"We hunted him. We were patient, at first, seeking to understand this new breed of danger," she sighed heavily. "But time passed and his safety at the heart of an army made it hard to do anything except try to mitigate his bloodlust. He pushed Jackson to kill more, brutalize more, and to offer no quarter. We made a play in Nashville, 1812; a fight broke out between Jackson and several of his officers. Askarii and I managed to get the bastard alone and we made our move."

Helen could *feel* the guilt filling the room, along with a grief so profound it threatened to consume the whole building.

"That's where Askarii, um, passed away?"

"Yes," Luciana turned around and Helen could see tears streaming down her perfect face. "Askarii led the charge, and she paid for it with her life. It was the first time I ever saw him *consume* another Fae. It was a nightmare I wouldn't wish on anyone. I barely escaped with my life."

She touched the claw-like scars on her body.

"Some of the forms he took, some of the powers he had," she shuddered. "I'd never before seen, nor have I since. The worst part is how much he *enjoyed* it. He evisc…he *eviscerated* her while she was still alive. He refused to kill her, and forced me to watch as he toyed with her. It's only because of her that I even managed to escape. She burned out every ounce of magic in her body to wound him—she tore a ragged hole in his face, and staggered him long enough for me to slip from his grasp."

Helen stood and embraced the guilt-ridden woman in front of her, wrapping her shaking body in a bear hug.

"I tried to go back for her, but he…he…he just–"

"Hey, hey," Helen squeezed tighter. "Hey, it's ok, I'm here. You did what you could."

"I tried to keep going, I tried again in 1876," Luciana's arms came up to loosely wrap around Helen's waist. "He was advising an officer called Marcus Reno. He convinced him not to intervene at Little BigHorn and got Custer and his men slaughtered. I thought maybe if I could *surprise* him, I could…He could've killed me then, he knocked me on my ass, blew a hole in my chest and then stood there, and just fucking *smiled* at me as I was bleeding out. He could've killed me but he knew, he *knew* it was worse for me to live."

"Oh Luciana, I'm so sorry. I…I don't know what to say."

"So I ran."

Just like you did.

Like you are.

"I ran and I hid, and I stayed hidden," Luciana's sobs wracked her body. "I'm a fucking coward."

"Hey," Helen said in a firmer tone. "You're *alive*, and I know that's what Askarii would want, it's *damn* sure what I want."

She stepped up on her tiptoes and gently kissed her lover.

"Thank you. Thank you for sharing more of your story with me, even though it's painful," she searched the woman's stormy eyes. "I…I'm no stranger to failure. I know the…*gnawing* feeling of it tearing at your whole being. I'm here for you."

"But now *you're* in danger," Luciana pressed. "Because of me. I've dragged you into this mess. My mess."

"Then arm me."

"What?"

"Arm me," Helen insisted. "Teach me. Tell me what I need to know, arm me with knowledge."

She paused, her expression one of earnest faith.

"I trust you."

Chapter Fifteen

"Wendigo?"

"Silver or iron."

"Lycanthropes?"

"Silver or wolfsbane."

"Naga?"

"Erm," Helen scratched at her cheek, deep in thought. "Uh, naga..."

Luciana frowned, her hands poised at the buttons of her shirt as she sat cross-legged in front of Helen.

"Hang on," Helen blurted out as Luciana started to pick up a sock off the floor and put it on. "Hang on, let me think for a second."

The two were sitting a few feet apart on the wooden floor of the cabin, passing time for the third day in a row since arriving in the blizzard. Luciana was wearing her underwear, the button-up shirt, a bra, and a stocking cap. The rest of her clothes were scattered around between them, a testament to how hard Helen had been studying the past few days.

"Uh," Helen groaned at last. "Fine, what are naga's weaknesses?"

"*Decapitation*," Luciana shook her head, pulling her sock back on. "You've got to learn these–"

"I know, they're the more common forms the Fae have taken in their lineages, they'll keep me alive, I *know*," Helen grumbled. "We're sure that a bazooka won't work? Or a chainsaw, or a…a woodchipper?"

"We're sure," Luciana half-smiled, her tone flat but with a hint of humor. "Ghosts and specters?"

"Salt."

"Good girl," Luciana purred, pulling the sock back off.

Helen's eyes widened. She felt her cheeks flush and squirmed a little at the unexpected praise.

Of course you have a praise kink.

What a fantasy—being good enough for someone.

"Shhh," she hissed to herself.

"Hmm?"

"Nothing, go on," she smiled.

"Pixies, nixies, and brownies?"

"Trick question, we don't kill young."

Luciana smiled and, rather than unbuttoning her shirt she slipped her panties off before tossing them to the side. Her shirt tails fell just *so*, hiding her most sensitive places from Helen's gaze but revealing enough to have her drooling.

"When you don't know what you're fighting, where do you start?"

"Iron."

The stocking cap came off next, much to Helen's chagrin.

"What's a fairy ring?"

"A place where Fae power is magnified," Helen recited dutifully. "Generally in the form of a mushroom ring."

Luciana lost the shirt.

Helen drank in the woman with unabashed obviousness. Her long, powerful legs that terminated in thick muscular thighs; the folds of her stomach as she sat, and the lines of her ab muscles running up both sides of her stomach to her fabric-encased bust; those strong arms propping her up; her powerful shoulders and delicate neck and collarbones; and of course the face that held her heart in a vice grip.

"Final question?"

Helen nodded dumbly.

"When are we safe?"

The question took Helen aback. She was fairly certain they hadn't covered this yet, but she also really, *really* wanted to see Luciana topless. She considered the threat they were currently facing, The Smiling Man, and opened her mouth to answer, pausing only at the last second.

What *would* happen after The Smiling Man was defeated?

Or kills you both.

Would Luciana go back to dragon hunting?

Of course she would.

Would she bring Helen with her…

Why would she want dead weight?

"Um…"

Helen's train of thought derailed over the answer. The obvious answer, the *only* answer.

"Never," she answered quietly. "We're never safe."

Luciana's face fell, her eyes a reflection of the sadness that Helen was feeling. She reached a hand across the intervening space and cupped Helen's cheek, brushing away a tear that Helen hadn't even felt.

"Yes, baby," her words were as soft as her skin. "So long as you're with me…so long as you exist in this world, you'll never be fully safe."

Helen leaned forward and planted a kiss on Luciana's lips.

"Safe is overrated."

She moved to pull away, but Luciana recaptured her lips with ease, falling forward onto her hands and knees and following Helen as she leaned back, eventually resting on the wooden floor with Luciana over her. Their kiss deepened and, as it did so, Helen found her legs wrapping around Luciana's waist. Luciana was nude, but Helen was hardly more clothed than that. She had a button-up of her own and a pair of boxer shorts—hardly an insurmountable barrier.

"The things I would do to you if I could use my magic," Luciana growled, sending lightning down Helen's veins.

"Who needs magic?" Helen smirked, bringing a hand between them and slipping her ring and middle fingers into her lover.

Luciana moaned softly as Helen's fingers curled inside of her, pushing on her g-spot while her palm pressed against her clitoris.

"Well," Luciana managed after a moment. "It's just that it's harder to *fuck* you the way I want to–why are you laughing?"

"Oh my poor, *spoiled* Fae," Helen pushed her back until she could sit up again, enjoying Luciana's confused face. "Stay."

Her command was met with wide, mischievous eyes.

"What are you doing?"

Helen traipsed over to her bag, pulling it open and retrieving something from within. Black leather straps and shining buckles contrasted nicely with the large, deep purple business end of her strap-on.

A single bag of possessions and how much space is occupied by sex toys?

"Toys and drugs," she smiled to herself as she slipped off her boxers and pulled the harness on.

This particular toy was her favorite, probably of all time. The harness was supple and comfortable, even for…extended use. It had a heavy, seven-inch member hanging off the front and a smaller but still filling five inch insert on the inside for the wearer—both of which had multiple vibration settings controlled by a small remote.

She finished buckling on the toy, sucking in her breath as the thick bulb of her end pressed against her tight opening before pushing it past her entrance where it filled her comfortably, then fishing around for the remote.

She didn't find the remote so much as she found a button on it, which immediately set the device pulsing softly inside her.

"Am I still staying?" Luciana pouted from behind her.

"Yes," Helen tried to keep her voice steady as she shut the vibration off and turned around.

Luciana was still on her knees facing the opposite direction, her ass resting on her ankles and her hands on her thighs.

"Oh you are good at following directions," Helen teased.

"I trust you're planning on making it worth my–*oh*!"

Luciana's eyes sparkled as Helen sauntered around to the front of her, drawing her hand across the back of the woman's shoulders as she did so.

"Who needs magic indeed," she smiled, leaning forward and running her hands up Helen's thighs.

Looking down at the beautiful, immortal, *magical* woman on her knees was a heady sight, and Helen's head swam with power. Her nerves were afire and she could feel herself clenching down on the toy inside her.

"We like?"

"We like," Luciana agreed vehemently, snaking a hand up and running it gently along the shaft as though Helen could truly feel it.

Helen's breath caught as Luciana leaned slightly back and snaked her free hand down between her legs, shamelessly pleasuring herself while keeping her eyes locked on Helen's. She leaned forward, peppering the inside of Helen's thighs with a thousand sweet kisses while she picked up the pace with her fingers below. Within a few moments, she was panting softly and her kisses had turned to nibbles.

"So do I have to beg you," she bit harder, probably hard enough to leave a mark. "Or are you going to fuck me?"

"I—"

Helen's thoughts trailed off as Luciana pulled back, turned herself around, and bent over. She placed her ass high in the air, wiggling it suggestively while laying the side of her face against the wood of the floor. With her legs spread, her lips were wide and her wetness was plain to see.

"Won't the floor hurt your knees?"

"We can only hope," she purred back.

Helen's face grew hot enough she felt certain that steam was escaping from her ears, but she obediently positioned herself behind the women, teasing her opening with the thick head of the strap-on.

"Helen?"

"Mhmhm," was all she could manage to answer.

"Don't be gentle."

Damn, the woman was going to get her to cum just by talking if she kept saying shit like that.

Helen watched as Luciana pushed back just hard enough to slip the tip inside herself, enjoying the reciprocating push of the other end of the toy.

She said don't be gentle, pussy.

Goaded by her lesser angels, Helen slammed her hips forward, burying the full length of the toy inside of Luciana.

Her lover gave a sharp cry, then quivered with pleasure just as Helen was about to ask if she was ok.

"Fuck yes," she breathed. "Like that plea-ah!"

Helen interrupted her with another hard thrust, pulling a sultry chuckle from the woman on the floor.

By the third and fourth thrust, Luciana was pushing back just as hard, her ass bouncing off of Helen's thighs with a loud, rhythmic smack. The sights and sounds of Luciana's pussy swallowing the large toy, paired with the pressure and pleasure of the bulb inside her own core, had Helen panting with exertion in no time. Every thrust forward set the harness rubbing against her own clit, the toy inside crushing against her g-spot, and her walls clenching down so hard they trembled.

"Ready for more," she whispered, not slowing down.

"M-m-more," Luciana questioned, her words more a moan than plain speech.

Helen tapped a few buttons on the remote, setting her own end of the toy into a gentle buzz and Luciana's into a strong, steady pulse.

"HoOly shit," Luciana began to shake. "They couldn't do thaaa-at in the sixties."

The quakes rocking Luciana didn't stop. Instead, her movements became even more erratic, until she was digging her nails into the floorboards and her toes were curling hard enough to pop. When the wave broke, it did so suddenly and with force. Luciana cried out and shook, *hard*, before falling to the floor trembling.

"Oh, f-fuck, Helen."

Helen laughed, clenching her thighs around the toy and teetering on the edge of her own orgasm.

"I don't think I can stand!"

"You don't need to love," Helen ran a hand through Luciana's sweaty hair.

"Ah, ah," Luciana smiled back. "It's your turn."

"There's not a lot you can do from down there," Helen pointed out.

"Lay back."

Helen complied and allowed Luciana to slip the harness off of her, gasping a little as the toy was pulled from within her. She felt empty, her over-eager pussy gripping on nothing as she craved to be filled again.

Luciana turned the harness around, holding the bulb that had been inside Helen and running the tip of the shaft across up and down Helen's vulva.

"I like where this is headed," Helen admitted.

Luciana took that as a sign and pushed the head of the toy inside her.

It was big, bigger than the end she'd been riding, and she felt herself stretch around it. But she was *hot*. She was as wet as she'd ever been and her body was begging for the rest of it.

"Hard or–"

"Hard."

Luciana's eyes sparkled as Helen blushed at her own eagerness.

But she didn't have long to stay shy. Luciana buried the toy, filling Helen just past the point where it hurt a little, then pulled it out halfway only to shove it back in. The hardwood floor dug into her shoulder blades and the grain pressed into her skin, but the toy more than made up for it.

Helen allowed her head to lay back, her whole body rocking with the force of Luciana's thrusts, and lost herself in the pleasure. The pulsing beat of the vibrations was still going, and it would've been plenty to set her over the edge, but Luciana wanted—or needed—more.

"Ah," Helen jerked as Luciana's tongue joined the fray, flicking across her clit unexpectedly.

Luciana was relentless.

She used her free hand to hold Helen's thighs open as she fucked her with the toy and danced circles around her clit. It took a minute or so but soon Helen's thighs were squeezing back against Luciana's strong hand and her back was arching off the floor.

She came. Hard.

But Luciana didn't let up until Helen's hands landed on her head.

As soon as Helen touched her hair, she lifted her head and paused her attentions.

"Ok," Helen sighed. "Ok, no more, I can't take any more."

Luciana smiled up at her, then gently removed the toy, tossing it aside before propping herself up on her elbows.

"See what studying gets you?"

"Where were you when I was in school," Helen sighed. "I wouldn't be dropping out if I had this kind of study-buddy."

They shared a laugh, catching their breaths, and lounging in the post-sex glow.

Both of the women nearly leapt out of their skins, however, when a loud banging sound echoed out through the cabin.

"California Highway Patrol," a loud voice called out. "Open up please."

"'Oh *fuck*," Helen hissed. "Oh fuck, oh fuck, oh fuck!"

She jerked on her button up and yanked her boxer shorts off the floor, nearly tripping as she stepped into them—backwards—and stumbled to the door. There was a tiny peephole and through it she could sure enough see a fifty-something year old man in a tan state trooper outfit, complete with a thick brown bomber jacket and a mustache any middle-aged dad would be proud of.

"Uh, um, one second sir," she called out, buttoning her shirt as quickly as she could.

She looked behind herself and saw Luciana wearing her bra and a pair of unbuttoned jeans, a long knife in one hand and her shirt in the other.

"Put that away, are you crazy," she hissed. "It's a cop!"

"Ma'am." the voice called out again. "I need you to open the door *now*, please."

"Uh, yes sir!"

She looked back again and the knife was nowhere to be seen. Luciana's jeans were now buttoned but she was still shirtless. She was looking around for her shirt but neither she nor Helen saw it.

"What do I do?"

"Just," Luciana looked around one last time then flung her arms across her chest. "Just open it."

Helen yanked the door open to reveal the stunned officer, one hand raised to knock again, and a slack-jawed expression on his face.

"Yes," she managed, crossing her legs and grateful her shirt extended most of the way down her boxers. "Yes sir, uh how can we help you?"

"Uhh…"

The officer looked past Helen, then back to her with a short, embarrassed cough that caused Helen to turn and follow his gaze–directly to the purple strap-on in the middle of the floor and her half-naked girlfriend.

"Uh," he sputtered. "We uhm, dispatch got a call of a vehicle up here from one of the regional, er, plow guys. There's not supposed to be anyone up here so I came to check it out."

"Y-yes," Helen tried her best to occupy more of the doorway. "We…got stuck in the snow! We were trying to get through the mountains when the snow hit, and this was the only shelter we could find."

"Uh yeah," he seemed as uncomfortable as she was. "Look it uh, it isn't the first time just…"

Helen didn't know what to say, so she simply kept her mouth shut and tried to ignore the blazing heat in her face.

"Uh, listen," the cop said. "I get it, you're um…*young*, and it's dangerous driving in the snow ah…I don't think anyone can fault you for using the facilities just um, well the roads are clear now, so you should be able to be on your way."

Another awkward silence.

"Uhm," he continued. "I think maybe I'll continue my patrol and just circle back around in an hour or so, make sure everything is back and locked up and such. Uh, just clean up, when…when you're…done."

"Mhmm," Helen squeaked. "Yes sir."

"Okey dokey," he gingerly tipped the brim of his wide hat and turned back down the steps toward his patrol car, which Helen noted was sitting in front of a large snow plow truck with flashing yellow lights.

Chapter Sixteen

Helen was still mortified, but the girls were still sharing spontaneous outbursts of belly-hurting laughter when they emerged from the mountains hours later.

"God, Luciana," Helen managed past another fit of giggles. "You should've seen the man's face—I think he was more embarrassed than we were."

Luciana, from her position in the passenger seat, was smiling back wryly while reading.

"And *you*! You had a friggin' *dagger*–"

"I don't know," she shrugged. "He could've been a threat!"

"I know, and don't get me wrong, that was hot," Helen nudged her. "But can you imagine what they'd say on the news?"

She did her best impression of a newscaster.

"Local sheriff knifed by half-naked burglars, suspects still at large, last seen driving a *station wagon* east..."

"Aw, I like the shaggin' wagon," Luciana patted the dashboard affectionately.

"It doesn't handle quite as well as it used to," Helen pointed out as they rounded one final curve before pointing the vehicle straight down into the plains.

"It has other perks."

Helen blushed at Luciana's mischievous smile.

"Easy tiger," she teased. "Or do you gain sustenance from pleasure in all its forms' too?"

"I spent twenty years in Rome as a succubus," Luciana flashed a wicked smile. "At the time it was a tactical decision, but I got pretty good at listening to confessions, too."

Helen blushed at the saucy wink she received.

You will never be enough for her.

"Tactical decision?"

"It made it a lot easier to manipulate humans," Luciana shrugged, reminding Helen with a single sentence how very different they were. "I needed resources, and I moved around a lot. Sex has always been the easiest and most powerful motivator for mankind."

"Rome," Helen was unexpectedly eager to change the subject. "Is that where you founded the Praetorian Club or whatever?"

"Uh, close actually," Luciana turned to face the window.

"What *is* the Praetorian Club?"

"It was an…agreement. We–"

"We?"

"Sorry, dragon hunters," Luciana explained. "It was a really rough time. We were coming out of the dark ages and so a whole bunch of us came together to create a club of sorts. The idea was we'd be able to keep tabs on each other, help each other out, pool resources, that kind of thing."

"So you made a John Wick assassin guild for immortal dragon hunters," Helen had to admit, that was pretty badass.

"Who?"

"Nevermind, it's a movie series you haven't seen yet."

"Ah," Luciana seemed to file away the name.

"So you said 'was' an agreement?"

"Yes, well," Luciana shrugged. "Initially, there were ninety-six of us, all on equal footing. We met in Constantinople—dragon hunters from *everywhere*. The best of the best. We set up a bunch of rules, invested our fortunes, and built something that was supposed to last—the global solution to dragons everywhere."

"That's pretty amazing, so what happened?"

"Well, one of the rules was no one in or out," Luciana laughed humorlessly. "No new Praetorians unless they were taking the seat of one who had fallen, and even then *only* if they were designated before they died. You could pass on your membership to a single person before your death and they would gain the perks of your…account."

"But then *you'd* lose them?"

"Correct."

"That doesn't seem like a good long term system…"

"It wasn't," she smiled. "Ironically, greed and pride kept most of us from passing on our membership and our numbers started to dwindle. Pretty soon ninety-six seats turned into less than half of that, and a whole lot of empty chairs at our meetings."

"You held meetings? Like…like the PTA, or the Freemasons?"

"The masons wish," she brightened a bit. "They were parties, really. Once a decade, we would gather and conduct business, party, burn out the stress and danger of our chosen professions. That lasted right up until the siege. Constantinople was attacked during one of our meetings in 1453. Three members died, several others were injured, and the meeting hall below the city was destroyed."

"But it's still a thing, right? I mean your card still works."

"Yeah, they moved to Switzerland, but some of us took exception to how…corporate it had become. We grew more concerned with hoarding wealth and power than we were with killing dragons."

"So you stopped going?"

"I stopped, Askarii stopped, another half dozen or so. As far as I know, the rest still meet, they must since my membership remains intact. Some of the folks had ideas about how to revive the group, make it more 'legitimate.' There was talk a while back about formalizing the passing on of a member's rights—some kind of squire-knight type deal, but I never bothered to dig into what came of it."

"Do you miss them?" Helen prompted. "Miss the meetings, the people, your colleagues?"

"I do, at times. A few I know have since died, even in my isolation I heard of their passing, but the rest…well, I doubt they would forgive me for leaving any more than I forgive myself."

They fell into silence as the mountains faded behind them. The ground around them was arid now, with shrubland and desert alternating as they passed through the southern Nevada desert. Miles passed in silence as Helen chewed on the newest information she'd gained about her partner.

An immortal dragon-hunting secret society wasn't *that* hard to swallow, thanks to Hollywood, but it was challenging to picture Luciana's fierce independence and go-anywhere attitude at a stuffy board meeting. She imagined a dimly lit dungeon below an ancient city, the walls lit by torches and deathly serious blood rites being conducted by robed figures centuries ago.

It didn't really compute.

“Do you want to switch out?”

“Hmm,” Helen snapped out of it. “No, I’m alright but I just realized I don’t actually know where we’re going.”

“We’re headed to sacred ground,” Luciana answered. “To Öngtupqa.”

“Sorry, to what?”

“The Grand Canyon, Öngtupqa,” Luciana laughed. “That’s what the Hopi called it. They were some of the earliest people to live there, possibly the first.”

“Ok, so what’s there?”

Helen tried not to let on how excited she was—she’d never been to the Grand Canyon before.

It’s a hole in the ground.

“It’s a waystation, a sort of sanctuary.”

“A sanctuary for anyone?”

“Yep, no blood can be spilled on sacred ground,” Luciana nodded. “All of the elders live on sacred ground and protect the sanctuaries.”

Helen balked, an elder?

Maybe you’ll have to wait outside like a pet.

"Do I..?" Helen started before rephrasing. "Am I allowed in?"

"With me you are."

Hot.

"So this elder–"

"Hashtaal Shash."

"Bless you."

"Very funny," Luciana was nonplussed. "Hashtaal is the elder who lives there. They've lived there since sometime before the seventh century, no one knows for sure."

"I thought there were no Fae here when you arrived?"

"Few, not none."

Helen rolled her eyes.

"Only a few Tom Bombadil types were here when I arrived," Luciana shrugged. "Some wanderers, some explorers, a few folks who came over with the norsemen, and a few who had been around longer—hell, for all I know Hashtaal came over on the land bridge."

Helen tried to imagine what someone as old as the last ice age would look like.

"So *why* aren't there any Fae native to the Americas?"

"That's a good question," Luciana answered. "As best I understand it, it's a combination of things. First, there *were* more Fae south of here, in Central and South America, than were found up in North America."

"Hmm, ok?"

"Remember that we Fae are linked to humankind in some…complicated ways," Luciana continued. "We cluster where people do—we thrive where they thrive. Some scholars think it's human belief that gave birth to us, and North America was less populous than Europe, Africa, and Asia at that time, only a couple of percent of the global population."

"I guess that makes sense, and the ones that *were* here?"

"That's another thing," Luciana's voice took a warmer tone. "The cultures here were so different. Europe especially had this attitude of conquering nature and overcoming the environment. Here the First Nations tended to have a much more peaceful, respectful relationship with the land. The Fae we found here reflected that, for the most part. They were kind, simple, gentle, shaped by the beliefs of the people who lived here."

"And this elder, is he more like that, or more like…you?"

If Luciana was any indication, he'd be gorgeous, powerful, and captivating.

"So this Hashtaal guy–"

"They're two-spirit."

"Ope, sorry."

Slick.

"But Hashtaal, you know them? Like, personally?"

"We met on many occasions," Luciana sighed wistfully. "Before the West was 'tamed', we spent many years in close contact. The elders swear oaths of neutrality, but often find a use for dragon hunters when it comes to protecting their chosen peoples."

"What about during the wars, like with Jackson?"

"The oath of neutrality is pretty strict. Hashtaal helped to steer and guide the First Nations, but could not intervene in their destruction. Ultimately, none of us proved more powerful than the imperialist war machine.”

They fell into another silence, Luciana reading while Helen cruised through the beautiful but barren landscape. Here it was easy to lose track of the fact that they were in modern day America—the sun-baked earth and wide open spaces felt ageless and raw. This was probably the same view the Hopi had centuries ago.

Minus the barbed wire fences and asphalt.

They skirted past Vegas, then cut across Arizona on their way east, the miles and hours clicking by as the sun wheeled overhead. They passed a highway marker indicating that they were nearing the Grand Canyon’s South Rim, it was less than a hundred miles. The scrubland turned from desolate and empty to desolate and sparsely inhabited. Helen cringed at the abject poverty she saw in every small collection of houses they passed. From the corner of her eye, she could see Luciana clenching her fists and she tried to think of what to say as sign after sign indicated this reservation or that, all named for near-dead communities and peoples that had been ravaged by America's violent past. And present.

"I'm sorry," Helen blurted out at last as they passed the fifth abandoned house in a row.

"Why?" Luciana's tone was clipped. "You didn't destroy these people's homes, their culture, or their livelihood."

"But I benefit from the system that did."

"You'd be amazed how many people fail to see that."

Luciana's voice was low enough that Helen wasn't sure the words were even intended for her, but she chose to respond.

"I've been fortunate, for the most part," Helen admitted. "Granted, being *crazy* hasn't done me any favors."

"In the middle ages, people who were crazy were often called touched by the Gods," Luciana snorted. "Their perspective and their wisdom was frequently sought out, unless their words pissed off the wrong church."

"Really?"

Helen was intrigued, this wasn't something she'd heard in history class.

"Sure. Seers, witches, shaman," Luciana waved a hand outside the window, encompassing the whole land around them. "Medicine men, wise women. They would be called crazy by today's standards, but back then—back when people *knew* there was more to the world than they could hear and see and touch—they were the rare few who could glimpse that unseen world."

"Maybe it's no coincidence your girlfriend is delulu."

"I assume that means delusional?"

Helen nodded, laughing.

"Maybe it isn't," Luciana shrugged. "My sister is an oracle, love, you assume I don't believe in fate?"

Helen took the woman's point and toyed with it in her mind. Maybe fate wasn't that far-fetched if a magical pornstar could foresee the future.

"I'm not sure I believe in fate," Helen decided at last.

"Oh?"

"I believe everyone is on a path," she started, working things out as she went along. "And I think the end of that path is foreseeable…but I think the path is malleable too. Like, you can change your destination by changing your choices, changing your path."

"Hmm," Luciana gave Helen's words clear and lengthy consideration. "I like that. I'm not sure I feel the same, but I like that quite a bit."

"What *do* you think about fate?"

"I think our destination is set, and the time of our death is predetermined, as are the general circumstances," she answered firmly. "But I think our conduct in the face of our trials, our challenges, and our deaths is up to us. It is incumbent upon us to face our fates with bravery, with dignity, and with conviction."

"So you think *I* am part of your *fate*," Helen wiggled her eyebrows in a comically suggestive way, drawing a smile from her partner.

"Very much so," she answered warmly.

Helen felt a warmth—like the glow of a low campfire—entering her soul.

"Speaking of our fate," Luciana continued, her tone cooling. "We need to talk about 'pursuit' and what we can expect after we check in with the elder."

"What do you mean?"

"Popping up on sacred ground is going to be noticed by a *lot* of other Fae," she explained. "Every major player has eyes on all the major enclaves, so you can expect that any interested party is going to know pretty well instantly when we show up."

"Meaning The Smiling Man."

"Exactly."

"Will he respect the neutrality of sacred ground though?"

"He'll have to," she nodded. "Not just because of our laws and customs, but because there's powerful magic laid down in those places."

Helen's mind started to wind up like a clockwork toy—like a tiny mechanical monkey crashing cymbals together. They'd run into him again, and god knew what else. More wendigo?

Wendigoes? Wendigo?
Wendigos…wendigoeses?

Worse?

"But we can stay there, right?"

Luciana answered with a subtle but noted shift of the question.

"We're safe as long as we're there," she nodded as though she'd answered the question. "But you can bet we'll be tracked the second we step foot off of sacred ground."

"Ok so—"

"Hey, we should pull off here for gas," Luciana interrupted. "This used to be the last gas station for a while, I don't know if that's changed."

Take a hint.

Helen tried to keep her face neutral despite her frustration that Luciana was very clearly avoiding the discussion she wanted to have. She felt her temper flare like a sunspot, the all-too-familiar sudden rage that sometimes accompanied her unmedicated periods. She tamped it down, refusing to allow her girlfriend to see that aspect of her personality.

Why not, she 'loves' you right?

Flaws and all?

As if someone could.

"Ok," she answered simply, turning on her blinker and pulling off the highway to a small waystation that saddled the empty road.

A small gas station with tan brick columns and touristy 'native' trappings was essentially the only open business in the small oasis. A drive-through liquor store and a small convenience mart stood there as well, but it was hard to tell from their dilapidated condition whether or not they were still in business.

"You pump, I'll be right back?"

"Sure."

Helen watched as Luciana beelined to the door, then unhooked the pump and swiped her card.

She's not telling you something.

"No shit," she grumbled.

The boredom of pumping gas had her looking around for distractions in moments, and her eyes caught on her backpack sitting half opened in the back of the vehicle. She couldn't see them, but she knew that just under the white t-shirt poking out of the bag was a plastic ziplock filled with pill bottles—bottles she hadn't touched in what, weeks now?

Tick tock goes the clock.

"I'm fine," she assured herself firmly.

"Hey," Luciana's voice pulled her eyes up and she noted that the woman had returned with a pair of dark gray plastic shopping bags. "I got snacks!"

The woman's smile was infectious, and by the time she'd hung up the pump and returned to the car she was well past her irritation.

"Catch."

Helen caught the off-brand cupcake.

"So," she announced as they both settled into their seats. "Are you uh, avoiding talking to me about something?"

Luciana paused, the cellophane crinkling in her hand as she gripped her own snack cake.

"Helen," Luciana looked up at her with a surprising amount of trepidation. "I'm…worried, about something, something I hope will not come to pass, but a part of me is afraid even to say it aloud for fear of speaking it into existence."

"Oh…"

"I guess I'm asking you to trust me, for now," she frowned and locked eyes with Helen. "Can you do that?"

No.

I can't even trust myself.

"Yes."

Chapter Seventeen

By the time they reached the entrance to Grand Canyon National Park, it was already dusk. The fading light illuminated a thick forest of pines, as well as rocky broken soil and the occasional elk or bison.

"It's changed so much," Luciana sighed.

"Since the sixties?"

"Since well before then," Luciana pointed at the wide empty valleys around them, with lush pastures and clearings. "These used to be *filled* with wildlife."

"There's some elk there," Helen pointed at a small group of animals laying down in a stand of trees, perhaps twenty individuals "That's–"

"Helen, the herds here used to be hundreds strong. Elk and bison filled the high prairies, while wolves and bear ruled the woodlands and the mountains," she sighed heavily. "Now there are *parking lots*, and a damned ice cream shop."

"I wish I could've seen this place back then," Helen admitted, trying to imagine how different the world must've been.

Luciana didn't answer, just stared out the window with a look of absolute heartbreak on her face.

The pair stopped eventually, after Luciana guided Helen to a place with an old wooden sign that said "Hermit's Rest Trailhead."

"Here's good," she announced as Helen pulled into the small lot. "We can head down to the sanctuary here."

"I don't think I can actually park here, This just looks like a turn-around."

"Not a problem," the woman unbuckled her seatbelt. "We're on sacred ground now—I can use magic."

"Oh," Helen hesitated, then followed suit, putting the car in park before clambering out.

"Grab your bag, if you need it."

Helen pulled her backpack from the backseat, swinging it comfortably onto her shoulders as Luciana moved to the front of the car. The woman raised her hands then brought them slowly together. As she did so, the car began to shimmer like a mirage or a too-hot asphalt road. Within seconds, it had utterly changed in its appearance. Where her modified station wagon had sat was now a large, rough boulder. It looked just as weathered and worn as any of the other stones in the area, though it was conspicuously in the center of the road.

"Sometimes the simple solution is the best one," Luciana smiled.

She moved her hands again, pushing them outward and to the side as the car-boulder slid sideways until it was just off the road. Now, with the vehicle sitting up against the rest of the jumbled stone and scrub beside the pathway, it looked just as natural as if it had been there for millenia. Hell, it blended well enough that Helen foresaw having a hard time finding it again when they were ready to leave.

Hopefully Luciana had some kind of magic GPS.

"You ready?"

Helen nodded in the affirmative and stepped lively to follow as she crossed a wide flat space and headed for the rim. They passed a kind of faucet set into the stone, with a plaque that indicated the water there was fresh and pure, straight from a mountain stream. Given that the pipe was metal and that there was no stream in sight, Helen had her doubts.

A few other hikers were heading in the opposite direction from them, all looking worse for wear but generally full of sweaty smiles and polite nods.

"You're not headed down now, are you?"

Helen turned around and found herself face-to-face with a park ranger. He had dark, tan skin and jet black hair that fell down past his shoulders. His accent indicated native ancestry and his face was painted with a kind of impassive concern.

"We are," Luciana stepped around Helen and fished a piece of paper out of nowhere. "We've got backcountry passes and wanted to beat the heat."

The man took the paper and looked it over carefully before returning it.

"There's a lot of switchbacks here," the man warned. "This is not an easy trail and in the dark it can be downright treacherous—not to mention cold enough to get icy. Take your time, know your limits, and remember that going down is optional, but coming back is mandatory."

"Thanks, ranger," Luciana smiled warmly, a soft, disarming southern drawl creeping into her voice. "We'll be careful."

The ranger's words echoed in Helen's mind as they got closer and closer to the edge of the canyon.

How dangerous is this trail?

When they finally hit the rim, Helen couldn't help but let out a low whistle.

That's a hell of a hole in the ground.

The canyon was indescribable. It was massive, and deeper than Helen had imagined. It wound around out of sight in both directions and it was so wide in places she could barely see the other side. The rocks had worn away over millenia under the pressure of a river she couldn't see—at the moment at least. What was left behind was a series of step-like layers, some of them hundreds of feet high. There were valleys and flat places on each level, and nothing but sheer rock and thin, terrifying switchbacks to take you from top to bottom.

"Jesus."

"You ok?"

"Yeah just," Helen swallowed her fear. "I don't think my brain really understood what the descent was going to be like."

"Tell you what," Luciana stepped behind her and wrapped her arms around Helen's waist, sending warmth rushing through her. "You be brave for me, and I'll rub your aching muscles later. Deal?"

Helen laughed, but she could feel her face heating up at the thought. Even so, Luciana's words poured warmth not just into her chest but into her heart as well. She took a deep breath, swallowing her fear and pushing back against the deep, reptilian part of her brain that was shouting 'this is a stupid fucking idea.'

What if I slip?

What if I jump.

Helen eyed the path leading down, it varied from about a foot to two feet wide and to call its outside edge a cliff was no exaggeration..

"Who goes first?"

"I will."

Whether she truly wanted to, or could read Helen's mind and feared for her intrusive thoughts,

Luciana stepped forward and onto the path just ahead of Helen.

"Come on," Luciana called out. "It'll be a few hours before we make it to the bottom."

Hours?

"Ok," Helen panted, "quick break."

Luciana paused dutifully, turning and wiping her own sweaty brow.

"You alright?"

"Yeah," Helen took her backpack off and slung it to the ground before leaning against the cliff wall. "I just didn't realize it was going to be so much work going *down*."

"Wait till we have to go up."

Helen groaned as she pulled her water bottle from her bag and took a long pull of the tepid water.

"And we can't just fly down, *why*?"

"It is tradition," Luciana smiled softly, then reached over and tucked a strand of Helen's hair behind her ear. "The canyon itself is warded, the journey is meant to inspire introspection, and it demonstrates the importance of the destination."

"That sounds like some old people shit." Helen grumbled as she picked her pack back up. "Some real 'back in my day,' and 'make the youngster hike uphill to school' type–"

Luciana's laughter cooled her annoyance as it echoed off the darkening canyon walls. They'd gone down through several of the step-like layers already, and they were nearing the river—or so Luciana kept telling her.

"It's right up here."

"So you keep sayin–oh wow," Helen stopped as they rounded a bend and the river came into view. "Oh Luciana, it's beautiful."

The river was wide and placid here, its slow waters running clear and clean over rocks and making soft, beautiful music as they did. Either bank of the river was covered in the vegetation that had been so lacking in the rest of the canyon. Even in the dark, it was plainly visible by the light of a full, pearly white moon.

"Come along," Luciana grabbed her hand and gave it a gentle tug. "We need to get to the cave, there'll be time for sightseeing in the morning."

"Just another moment?"

"Alright," Luciana relented. "Just one more."

Her reluctance was barely tone-deep, and Helen felt her own desire to stay out in the cool, beautiful night. Luciana's arm slipped around Helen's shoulders and she felt herself pulled close. Luciana's warm lips brushed gently across the top of her head and for a moment the pair simply stood staring at the water, and the stars, and moon reflected in it.

"Come on," Luciana said after a moment. "We have company."

"What?"

"To the left, across the–"

The second half of her sentence was cut off by Helen's sharp intake of breath. How in god's name had she missed the *enormous* bear sitting perched on a flat, table-like rock. The animal was huge, bigger than a car. and in the night it looked like a shadow-against shadows with huge muscles, thick, shaggy fur, and bright inquisitive eyes.

"Luciana," she squeaked softly. "What do we do?"

"We don't *do* anything, love," she felt the woman's arm squeeze her shoulders gently. "Come on."

Helen hesitated as Luciana turned away, but in the end she could do nothing but trust her partner.

"But–"

"In good time."

Luciana picked through the quiet night without making so much as a rustle against the stones, whereas Helen's feet were less sure. Not to mention that Helen was following as closely as she dared, the bear still fresh in her mind.

They hadn't walked ten minutes more when they came to a wide cave entrance set into the wall of the canyon. Helen felt a now somewhat familiar tugging at her heart, and in the distant places of her mind she would swear she could hear wind rushing through tall grasses and the beating of faint drums.

"Welcome to the sanctuary," Luciana whispered softly, taking in a deep breath and then letting it slowly out. "Welcome to Öngtupqa."

Luciana took her hand once more and gently pulled her forward into the darkness.

The bottom of the cave was thick, soft sand, which was good because the interior was the darkest black that Helen had ever experienced. It seemed like they'd walked for ages, but nothing at all changed as far as Helen could tell. She would've asked her lover, but what was there to ask that wouldn't sound an awful lot like 'are we there yet?'

"You may feel a bit of resistance here," Luciana cautioned her. "Don't worry."

"What–"

Helen felt suddenly as though she'd walked into a curtain of jello. The air around her grew so thick that it physically prevented her travel. She opened her mouth to speak but realized she hadn't the faintest idea what it was she'd been about to say.

"Luciana, I…"

Where am I?

What are we doing?

Ah, that's right, she reminded herself, we came in here to explore the cave and found nothing—what a shame, maybe the rest of their journey would be more eventful.

"Well, I guess we should head back," she mumbled, blinking in confusion as she turned back the way she'd come.

"Helen."

"Come on, we can make it back to the car by dawn if we try–"

"Helen, come on, we're almost there."

"What do you mean?" Helen laughed. "We've already looked, there's nothing here."

"*Look again.*"

Helen closed her eyes.

"*Look. Again.*"

A pinprick of light shone through her closed eyelids, a warm glow of orangish red that flickered and danced as it grew.

Her eyes flickered open and she blinked in surprise, her eyes watering at the unexpected light of a roaring campfire.

"What the–"

"It's an enchantment, love," Luciana patted her gently on the back. "Meant to keep out curious mortals."

"It nearly worked," Helen admitted, shaking the lingering feeling that they'd fully explored the cave and found nothing but smooth stone at the back, despite the evidence to the contrary in front of her own face. "I would *swear*."

"Well, it wouldn't be much good otherwise," Luciana nudged her. "Come on, have a seat."

Luciana gestured at the warm sand that surrounded the bright but smokeless fire. They were in a small cavern—easily comfortable enough to fit a dozen people spread out on the sand. There were sleeping bags strewn about, as well as a few stumps that had been positioned around as seats.

The space was empty except for one sleeping bag near the back, which looked to have an occupant but the person was facing the other way.

"Come on."

Helen took a seat next to Luciana, who dropped her bag next to a pair of sleeping bags off to the side and then sat facing the fire.

"Luciana," a deep, soft voice intoned from behind them. "It has been many years, child."

"Hashtaal," Lucian stood and turned, answering brightly. "By the moon, it is good to see you, elder."

"And you have brought a friend, a *mortal* friend."

Helen followed Luciana's movement and found herself looking at an *ancient* native man with skin like deeply creased leather and stark white hair in a braid down his back. He wore a simple brown cloak over his bare chest, and a pair of buckskin pants to complement his bare feet.

"Greetings, Helen of Tennessee."

"Y-you know me?"

"I do," he nodded solemnly. "The birds and the trees speak of a troubled girl far from home. The winds speak of a young woman who survived a wendigo, one who roused a mighty dragonhunter from centuries of isolation."

Reverence filled her and she stood in awe of the man and his deep, obvious connection to the earth.

"The *winds*?"

"Tetiana called me," the old man laughed. "Come, have some supper."

Hashtaal led the way to the campfire and indicated the two women should sit.

Helen felt the ground and was pleased to find the sand was soft and didn't seem to stick to her, despite her sweaty condition. She took her seat and turned her attention back to the elder.

The elder was bent over a large clay pot—a cauldron, for lack of a better term—and was stirring the contents gently while humming softly.

"Vegetable soup?"

"Yes, please," Helen piped up, despite a look from Luciana.

"You must be hungry," he pulled a small ceramic bowl from thin air, filled it with a ladle, and then handed it to her. "After such a long trek."

"Starving," Helen admitted, finding that it was true even as the words left her mouth.

"Elder," Luciana spoke up, her tone urgent. "We–"

"It can wait, child," Hashtaal shook his head and laughed. "You have always been eager. Have some soup."

Luciana grumbled but relented, taking her own bowl and immediately setting it down in the sand beside her.

"Helen," Hashtaal smiled. "Tell me, how did you come to be in Luciana's…orbit?"

"Her orbit," Helen smiled at the peculiar turn of phrase. "Uh well, I actually crashed into her bridge."

"She has a way of drawing one in," the man's eyes sparkled. "Something I have always admired in her. I trust that, since you are here, you survived your crash without issue?"

"Yes, uh, elder," she felt the need for the honorific, despite his pleasant tone.

"And after you recovered, what kept you near?"

She trapped me?

"Ah," she coughed softly, then cleared her throat. "Inclement weather prompted her to extend her hospitality."

"And then?"

Does he know?

He can't know.

Can't he?

"And then she tricked me," Helen's smile flattened. "And kept me at her home under the impression that I couldn't leave."

"I see," his eyes saddened, but he never broke contact with Helen's gaze.

Helen snaked a hand toward Luciana and their fingers found each other even without looking.

"S-she apologized," Helen clarified. "And I've forgiven her. Water under the bridge."

"The broken bridge," Hashtaal's eyebrows rose. "Or a different one, I wonder?"

"She fixed the bridge," Helen answered firmly.

"Ah," the smile was bright again, though it didn't fully reach the elder's eyes. "But here I am pestering you, how impolite of me."

"There is no debt," Helen ventured, pulling a more genuine smile from them.

"You learn our ways quickly," they laughed. "But come, you must have questions, no? It is my role to be a teacher, as much as a guardian."

"I can ask anything?"

"You may, though I might not answer."

Slippery.

"What is this place, exactly?"

"This is a sanctuary, one of many positioned around the globe in this realm and in others," Hashtaal explained. "And it has been my home for many human lifetimes."

"Why are there sanctuaries?"

"War."

Helen waited for the elder to expand, but they seemed content with their answer.

"So the sanctuaries prevent war?"

"That is the hope, distilled to its simplest form, yes."

"And this place is a sanctuary to Fae and humans both?"

"It is a sanctuary to all creatures great and small, to all life," he glanced around them. "No blood can be spilled here."

"Not even an ant? Or a flea?"

"None."

"What about the plants? Aren't they alive?"

"I had forgotten how curious humans are, it has been many centuries since one of your kind ventured here."

Not an answer.

"Easy," Luciana murmured beside her, squeezing her hand softly.

"Forgive your friend her questions," Hashtaal reassured the woman. "You had many questions, once upon a time."

"Can you tell me what it was like, back then?"

"When Luciana arrived, or before?"

"Before, when *you* first came to this place."

"Very well," Hashtaal smiled, spinning the tale despite Luciana's obvious surprise. "The land was young, and ice and snow still covered much of the lands north of here."

Some time later, Hashtaal politely paused as Helen stifled the latest in a series of massive, jaw-cracking yawns.

"I'm so," another yawn. "I'm sho shorry."

Helen rubbed the sleep from her eyes and took another sip of the cool, refreshing tea that the elder had provided. The beverage, poured from a clay pitcher into small wooden cups, tasted faintly of pawpaw, pear, and agave. It perked her up, but even the light, fruity beverage couldn't hold back the blanket of exhaustion forever.

"You are tired, child," Hashtaal's deep smile lines creased as they graced her with a knowing look. "There will be time for more history in the morning. It is nearly dawn now, and you must rest."

Helen yawned again, then nodded as Luciana led her to one of the sleeping bags.

"Thank you, elder Hashtaal."

They might've answered, but Helen was asleep before her head hit the pillow.

Chapter Eighteen

"How *dare* you enter this sacred space!"

Luciana's poisonous tone pulled Helen from her sleep instantly.

She sat bolt upright, the sleeping bag bunching around her waist as she took stock. Luciana was standing protectively in front of her, looking across the cave at-

Him.

The Smiling Man was unmistakable. His form was hunched ever so slightly within the confines of the cave, but it did nothing to diminish the cold rock in Helen's gut. His suit was immaculate, despite the dusty conditions, and the darkness of the cloth made his pallid flesh stand out even more. He was an unnatural presence here, and the cave around them was colder, emptier, less *alive* in his presence.

The thing's eyes, or the hollow pits that served as such, were trained on Luciana, but Helen was not naive enough to think he didn't notice her as well. His cracked, chapped lips were stretched wide and his gruesome yellow teeth were on full display.

"Whatever do you mean?" he teased softly, a tone like a viper's poison running through his words. "All are welcome in the sanctuaries. Or are you so removed from our ways that you have forgotten this most basic tenant?"

His gaze flicked to Helen.

"Or perhaps your time among mortals has eroded your manners."

"Leave her out of it," Luciana growled.

"Come now," he smiled wider, his lips oozing dark red blood where they split from the strain of his skin. "Your pet is welcome here too, no need for such…*hostility.*"

Luciana took a step forward but was stopped mid-stride by Hashtaal's harsh voice.

"There will be peace in this sanctuary," the man wasn't shouting, but his words reverberated against the stone walls loudly enough to set Helen's vision off. "The two of you *will* abide by the sacred laws. Your quarrel is moot here–"

"Elder, Hashtaal, you cannot be serious!"

"Can't he," The Smiling Man snapped. "Your words border on insult, hunter."

"Then I have not made my feelings clear enough," Luciana hissed back.

"You know, I recall a similar conversation the last time you and Askarii–"

"Do not speak her name!"

The Smiling Man laughed, though if Helen had not seen it with her own eyes she would have believed the sound to be a tortured crow calling for the release of death. The noise did not linger, did not carry, rather it ended in an unsettlingly abrupt fashion—like a grape that had shriveled on the vine.

"You cannot hide here forever, little hunter," he prodded at her. "Surely you haven't forgotten that along with your manners?"

"Enough," Hashtaal interrupted at last, standing from where he knelt beside the fire. "There will be peace and *decorum* in my sanctuary. If the two of you cannot be civil, you will both be banished from this place."

"Of course, elder," The Smiling Man gave the barest hint of a deferential nod, but did not turn to acknowledge the elder's words. "I was simply passing through and thought to pay my respects—it has been an *age* since last we saw each other, hasn't it Hashtaal? And how pleasant for me to meet another old acquaintance, what a lovely happenstance."

Helen could feel the anger radiating off of her lover like heat waves from molten lava. She unconsciously curled herself tighter into a ball, pulling her knees to her chest as the two faced off a moment longer.

When The Smiling Man moved at last, it was with an exaggerated slowness, a lazy, 'you wouldn't dare' walk that carried his ungainly, horrifying form toward the entrance of the cave. He paused just outside of the firelight, his hunched, elongated form half hidden in shadows.

"I'll be seeing you soon, hunter."

The moment he disappeared into the darkness Luciana rounded on the elder, her hackles still raised.

"How could you allow him here?" she growled. "Have you no *shame*? Have you no regard for our brothers and sisters who suffered and died—no, worse than died, were *consumed* by that monster?"

Hashtaal was calm in the face of her anger, but Helen could see lightning flash in his eyes when he answered her.

"You forget yourself," his low gravelly voice stilled the air in the room. "I will obey the sacred laws in all things, but most especially with regards to this sanctuary. Your own welcome is in as much jeopardy as his—you would do well to remember that no matter our history and our ties, you abide here at my whim."

"But–"

"I will do what I must to protect this place, Luciana," he raised a finger to cut her off. "Perhaps you would do well with some fresh air."

Helen scrambled to her feet as Luciana stormed off toward the entrance. She cast a quick glance at Hashtaal, but the elder was already tending to the fire, his back turned to the retreating women.

"Luciana," she called out softly, then again louder. "Hey, Luciana, wait for me!"

Helen was huffing and puffing by the time she caught up to Luciana near the entrance to the cave.

"Hey," she caught her breath as they stepped into the daylight together. "What the hell, you can't just go storming off like that."

Lucian turned back long enough for Helen to see tears on her cheeks and all of her irritation melted away instantly.

"Hey, whoa, are you ok?"

She reached for Luciana but the woman was already walking away, arms wrapped around herself tightly and shoulders hunched.

Helen followed her quietly as she made her way from the cave to the river's edge and then along it. They walked for several minutes before Luciana paused a few feet from the water.

Tentatively, unsure whether or not it was the right thing to do, Helen walked up behind the taller woman and wrapped her in a hug.

Luciana melted.

Helen could feel the woman's body trembling and, as she lay the side of her head against Luciana's back, she could hear her ragged breaths.

"How can I show that I care?"

"Sit with me?"

"Of course."

Luciana sat in the dust beside the river and Helen popped down beside her before slipping an arm around her waist.

"Do you want to talk about it?"

"I…this place, and *him*, it just…brings back a lot of painful memories."

Helen waited quietly for Luciana to continue, unsure if she should say anything herself.

"You said you wanted to see this place the way I did," Luciana raised her head and sniffled, a strange, determined look in her eyes. "Do you still want to?"

"What do you mean?"

"I mean I *can* show you, if you want."

"S-sure," Helen stammered, a little wary of what she was agreeing to. "Yeah, yes, I'd love to."

"This'll feel pretty intense," Luciana raised her hand, her index and middle fingers joined, and set them gently against Helen's temple. "Just remember none of it is real, or rather…it all happened long ago."

"I–"

Helen drew in a sharp breath as the fingers against her head turned cool and her vision swam.

Helen's vision returned a split second later, but it was…different. The world around her was relatively unchanged save for a very slight sepia tone that seemed to have fallen over everything. That and her senses were…dull. She could still see, hear, taste, smell, but everything felt filtered and, for lack of a better term, *sad*.

This is the last time I was here with her.

Helen felt herself 'jump' at the disembodied voice, but her body didn't move.

Wait, was it even her body?

She tried to look around, to move, but her vision was focused forward on the other side of the river, and her limbs did not respond. She felt a spike of panic flow through her mind, but immediately a wave of reassurance followed.

It's ok. You're in my memory now. You're safe.

Helen took the mental equivalent of a shaky breath and tried to relax.

"Amanar!"

Helen/Luciana turned at the sound and a warmth spread into her mind as her eyes landed on a radiant woman that she immediately recognized as-

"Askarii," the words came from her, but they were unmistakably Luciana's voice."

Amanar?

The name I used back then.

Her clipped reply gave Helen two distinct impressions: There was a story there, and she wasn't ready to share it.

Askarii was fit, lithe, and wore her hair shaved nearly to her scalp. Her dark skin made a perfect pairing for the beadwork and turquoise on her dark blue dress. She wore moccasins and deerskin leggings beneath the dress, which was clearly made with love and custom fitted to her.

"Welcome back, love," Helen balked at the kiss the two women shared, jealousy warring with the overwhelming flood of serotonin and love she felt for the woman. "How'd it go?"

"Hashtaal is stubborn," Askarii laughed, taking Helen/Luciana's hand and leading her back to the water. "He always has been."

"Will he join us though?" they pressed. "Will he help us fight–"

"No," Askarii heaved a heavy sigh. "He stands by his neutrality, no matter the rumors surrounding The Smiling Man's newfound power."

"Damnit."

"It's alright," Askarii laughed—a charming, warm sound that sent butterflies into Helen/Luciana's stomach. "We've fought worse and won."

"Your optimism never ceases to amaze," they answered her, looping their arms around the woman's waist and pulling her in for another kiss.

"With you," Askarii broke their kiss long enough to reply. "What else could I be *but* optimistic?"

Their kiss deepened and Helen felt herself growing flush. She could feel Luciana's body responding, and her mind could feel everything just as clearly. Her arousal peaked and she felt closer to reality the more *engaged* their shared body became.

"Harlot," Askarii whispered into her neck as her lips moved from their lips to their ear, then down to their collarbone. "You'll have us naked in the noonday sun if you have your way."

"What of it?" Luciana giggled, nibbling at Askarii's ear and giving her rear a playful squeeze. "There's no one here but us."

Helen's vision swam again, disorienting her as she remembered that she wasn't really herself, wasn't really there. Her thoughts didn't even have time to clear before her vision resolved itself into another of Luciana's memories—this time in a less familiar scene.

She was standing a few feet from the edge of the canyon, with the cliffs to her back and Askarii by her side.

The Smiling Man was standing in front of them, about thirty feet ahead. There were two bodies at his feet, and a young native girl was struggling in his grasp. She couldn't have been past her teens, and she looked especially small as he held her aloft with one hand at her throat and her feet kicked uselessly in the air.

"Put her down," Askarii growled, gripping the spear she held in her hands.

"Or else what?" he drawled. "You'll *hunt me down*?"

He laughed the same raspy, horrid laugh.

"You would protect these hunters," he accused, his tone dark and every syllable sharp and jagged. "They would *kill* you, given the chance."

"They're just doing what they–"

Luciana's words were cut off with a sickening crunch as the man crushed the girl's windpipe in his hand, immediately causing her body to fall still.

Askarii's spear was like lightning, whipping across the thirty feet, and lodging deep in The Smiling Man's chest. The blade sank deep into his flesh and his body jerked from the impact, staggering back a step before righting himself again.

"Adorable," he cackled, dropping the young girl to the ground and bemusedly regarding the spear in his chest.

How?

I wish I knew. I wish I'd known…

"You have nothing that can hurt me," he pulled the spear out and lazily tossed it to the ground between them.

"Everything dies," Askarii spat. "Even a thing like you has a weakness."

"There is nothing else like me," The Smiling Man's retort was acid, his voice rising to an unhinged yell. "There never has been before, and there never will be again."

He took a step forward, ignoring the now three bodies at his feet.

"The only reason you're alive is because I have thus far found you amusing," he hissed. "Or perhaps you'll step outside that sanctuary and test that theory?"

Helen could feel the tension in her body, could feel Luciana's muscles trembling and twitching to fight, to strike.

"Exactly," The Smiling Man sneered. "All bluster, as with all the hunters before."

"You should know our record for killing dragons–"

"I am no dragon," he snarled. "Do not compare me to those weak, insipid pretenders you've killed. I am above them, beyond them."

"You are just another abomination."

The Smiling Man stepped forward again, then pointed at the ground. A line appeared in the dust and rock, a near straight streak of darkness that marked the edge of the sanctuary.

"Then come out and play."

Askarii started forward and Helen/Luciana felt herself reach out and grab Askarii's arm.

"Amanar?"

"Don't," they answered. "Not here–"

"He's *killed* innocent people," Askarii's eyes were wide with betrayal. "Just now, just feet away he's spilled innocent blood right in front of us and you're what…you want to back down?"

"I don't want to," their murmured response was low and earnest. "But we've got no–"

"We've got no what, no advantage?" Askarii shook her head. "You'd risk the lives of more innocents if he walks away from here when we could stop him *now*?"

"Askarii, my love–"

"Don't," Askarii jerked her arm away and refused to meet their gaze.

"Aw," The Smiling Man hissed darkly. "Trouble in paradise?"

"And you," Askarii rounded on the man, stepping right up to the line. "Your days are numbered."

"I tremble with fear," he goaded. "How ever shall I sleep at night?"

Askarii spat at the man's feet, the glob of saliva landing on his fine shoes.

"Charming," his voice turned dark with irritation. "I'll be seeing you soon—both of you."

Without another word, the man raised a hand and disappeared with a sharp crackle like thunder.

"Askarii, please."

"Amanar," her raised hand warded off their attentions. "I don't know who you are anymore. The woman I love wouldn't stand to watch innocents die, no matter the risks."

"He is *strong*, and *dangerous*!"

"As are they all!"

"We have to do this right," they yelled. "I can't lose you."

"Perhaps not," Askarii started walking away. "But every drop of blood he spills from now on out is on your hands, on *our* hands."

Ouch...Luciana, do you–

There's one more thing I need you to see.

Are you sure?

Luciana's answer came in the answer of another jarring, swirling change in scenery. This time they were face down on their hands and knees in the dirt. Helen felt a searing pain in her chest and stomach, and could taste copper in her mouth. Her body looked down at the dark red blood dripping from her stomach and her mouth, hitting the ground with a steady splatter.

Breathing hurt, their heartbeat was weak and erratic, and the edges of her vision were flickering in and out of blackness.

"Oh Amanar," The Smiling Man's raspy voice made his sing-song tone all the more disturbing.

Helen/Luciana drew a painful breath before a wracking cough tore through their body. When the coughing fit subsided, there was more blood on the ground–but they pulled themselves along, one hand clutching their wounded stomach and the other in the dirt.

They could see the edge of the Grand Canyon in front of them—close, but much too far.

"Now now, don't *leave*," The Smiling Man sang out as his dress shoes appeared at the edge of their vision. "We aren't done playing, are we?"

A searing pain wracked their torso as a spear—Askarii's spear—sprouted from their chest, staking them to the ground as it impaled them. They felt a lung collapse and a sizzling, burning pain from the silver and gods-knew-what-else imbued within the spear, it tore at their flesh and sent waves of pain rippling down their nerves.

"Just do it," they managed to speak, each word pulled from a hoarse, ragged throat but nonetheless laced with defiance. "Kill me."

"Oh my dear, stoic huntress," a long-fingered hand reached down and gripped their chin, the cold, clammy flesh making their skin crawl even through the pain. "Where's the fun in that?"

Horror gripped them.

"I'm not going to kill you. Not yet, anyway," he whispered. "Not when it's so much more…enjoyable to witness your *delicious* suffering."

"No," Luciana's tone was dangerously close to begging. "Just do it, finish it."

"When you die—*when I kill you*—it will be at my leisure," he knelt down beside her, hot fetid breath that reeked of rotting meat blowing across her face. "And I will take *great* pleasure in it. But kill you now, at the height of your pain? That would be a mercy, am I known for my mercy, little huntress?"

They were silent, torn between passing out and vomiting from revulsion.

"No, I think not," he answered for her. "You dared to hunt me, *me*! Now you will pay for your stupidity."

She watched his forked tongue roll across his lips as he smiled down at her.

"I think I shall continue to kill the ones you love, to hunt down every shred, every *scrap* of your happiness and rip it from your life. You will suffer until you beg me for death and still, even then, I will deny you."

Chapter Nineteen

Helen fell back into herself like fine china hitting a brick wall. She gulped air like a drowning man, clutching her chest with both hands, feeling for the wounds and the blood. Her hands shook as she clutched at her stomach, her throat, all the places The Smiling Man's cruelty had marked.

But there were none.

She was safe.

Even so, she couldn't breathe. Her lungs wouldn't fill and fire burned in her blood like battery acid.

"Helen," Luciana's hands gripped her shoulders, sending her into a panic.

She pushed back instinctively and, despite the woman being significantly stronger than she was, she found herself instantly free of Luciana's grasp.

"I'm sorry," the woman's eyes were wide and apologetic, her hands hovering a few inches off of Helen's skin. "I...I don't know how to help."

Helen was finally able to pull air into her lungs with a hoarse, ragged croak.

"I'm ok, I'm ok, I'm ok," she repeated herself endlessly, unsure of who she was trying harder to convince.

"I'm sorry, that was too much," Luciana frowned, water streaking down from the corners of her eyes. "I–"

Helen interrupted her with a massive bear hug, heedless of the fact that they were both still sitting in the dust beside the river.

"This is real, right?" Helen whispered, her eyes scrunching shut and her focus honing in on her lover's breathing, her heartbeat, and the feel of her sun-warmed skin. "This is real? Not a memory, or a dream or…anything else?"

"This is real."

Don't you usually tell yourself that?

Helen opened her eyes again. Less than a foot separated their faces, and Helen could pick out the individual grains in the dust clinging to the streaks of moisture on Luciana's face.

"Luciana, I'm…I'm so sorry."

"Sorry? What do you have to be sorry for?"

Helen noted the cooler, more collected filter coming down across Luciana's face and raced to beat it.

"I'm sorry that happened to you."

"I made mistakes," Luciana cast her gaze downward. "And I paid for them, *continue* to pay for them."

"Luciana, what happened wasn't your fault," Helen pushed. "Even knowing only a small piece of the picture I can see that–"

"Helen, my actions led to that outcome, to Askarii's death, and to countless others since then, and I hid from the consequences of my actions."

"Hey–"

"Helen, I have spent decades, *centuries*, in isolation," Luciana pulled back slightly further. "Because Fae can't lie, and when he told me he'd hunt down anything and anyone that made me happy he…well, he meant it. He meant it and he's made good on it."

Helen's face fell.

Does this sound like goodbye to anyone else?

"I broke that isolation, and in so doing I put *everything* you have *ever* worked for in jeopardy. Your life, your future, both are in danger because of my selfishness."

"Hey, I walked into this with eyes wide open, remember?"

"Did you? Couldn't I have just as easily fixed your car and sent you on your way?"

"Well," Helen sputtered. "I meant after I found out that you're a witch."

"Which again was *my* choice to reveal to you."

"Don't do this."

"Helen, I have allowed myself to live without experiencing true joy for a long, long time," Luciana looked down to her lap. "It's the safest way to live—the safest for me and certainly the safest for anyone I could care about. I cut off friends, the closest thing I have to family–"

"Wait," Helen's heart was in her throat.

"Helen," Luciana's eyes drifted back upward and locked with her own. "I convinced myself that living without happiness was the price I was paying for my sins."

Here it comes.

"But I can't live like that, like *this*," Luciana pushed back and stood, turning her back to Helen and pacing the ground. "Cutting myself off from the life force of my people, from *emotion*."

Wait, what?

"Helen, I don't *want* to suffer in silence," she turned back, her eyes sparkling with fiery intensity. "I can't. I won't put my heart back on a shelf. Life is short, even for my kind, it is not forever, and for yours it's a brief but brightly burning flame. I don't want to spend it hiding, I want to spend it–"

Luciana paced, leaving little puffs of dust behind with every step as her speed increased. She wasn't looking at Helen now, instead she was looking at the ground, talking as much with her hands as with her lips.

"I want to spend it walking, and eating fine foods, and tasting wine," she continued, ranting now. "I want to travel, to wander, to see unfamiliar mountains at sunset and wake up on dew-covered grass."

She stopped pacing.

"I want to spend it kissing the girl I want to kiss," her eyes linked back with Helen's and she took a step closer. "I want to feel your heartbeat against mine, I want to savor every second, relish every experience, and, damnit Helen, I want to *live* again."

Helen blinked rapidly, torn between shock and awe as Luciana gingerly extended a hand to her where she was still sitting on the ground.

"I–"

But the words wouldn't come.

So she did the next best thing—she took the offered hand and allowed Luciana to effortlessly pull her up from the dirt and into a firm embrace.

"Luciana, I just," her lips captured her lover's and her words turned breathy as she interrupted herself. "I thought you…were going to tell me you're leaving me…and you…drop *that*? The most epic…end-of-the-movie…rom-com monologue?"

Luciana was laughing before Helen could even get her entire sentence out, making their kissing even more challenging than Helen's talking alone.

"I'm sorry–"

"Don't be."

"Damnit, woman," Luciana groaned as she set her hands on Helen's hips and lifted her off the ground, turning them in a slow circle while Helen wrapped her legs around the woman's waist. "You're an addiction I couldn't kick if I wanted to, and I don't want to."

"So I'm stuck with you," Helen draped her arms over Luciana's shoulders and squeezed tightly with her legs.

"Yes, you're stuck with me."

"Good," Helen felt the emotions held in her taut muscles warming and turning to a different sort of desperation. "You're stuck with me, too."

"That so?"

"Mhm-ahahahaaaah," Helen burst out laughing as Luciana took the gentle sway of their kissing and instead spun Helen around in a circle before backing her up against the canyon wall.

The warm red rocks pressed against her flesh and Helen couldn't help but think of the woman's nails running down her back. She trembled with excitement as her body trauma-dumped her fear and anxiety into arousal.

Luciana must've felt the same, because Helen could feel the heat pouring off of her like a furnace.

Helen's hands roved across Luciana's back, then tugged up on the hem of her shirt. The garment slipped off so easily that Helen suspected it might've had magical help. The woman's bra came next, the expensive fabric snagging on a prickly cactus as it was thrown haphazardly over her shoulder.

Helen bent down to celebrate her lover's newly exposed skin, then gasped in a mix of pain and pleasure as Luciana shoved her firmly back against the rocks. The taller woman's lips danced across her neck and collarbones, pulling a moan from Helen's parted lips.

Luciana's hands squeezed her ass firmly, then worked their way up to her chest where they tore open her shirt with a savage strength that sent shivers between Helen's legs.

Helen found that the buckle of Luciana's belt situated perfectly so that, by pressing her back to the stone, she could grind her vulva across the hard metal.

The pressure was delicious.

She found her rhythm, rocking her hips and digging her fingernails into Luciana's powerful shoulders as the pleasure built between her legs.

"Wait, um, Helen?"

She froze.

"I'm sorry, can we…" Helen opened her eyes and held herself back, stuck awkwardly tangled around the woman. "Can we go a little slower, this time? A little–"

"Gentler?"

Luciana nodded, a strange vulnerability evident in the distance in her eyes.

"Of-of course!"

Luciana set her gently back on the ground, then took a half-step back looking sheepish.

"Sorry, did I kill the–"

Helen interrupted her doubts with a softer, slower, but just as passionate kiss. She gently set her hands at Luciana's waist and kept her hunger in check.

"D'you think you could–"

Luciana snapped her fingers and a wide sarape rustled into existence on the ground beside them. The fabric of the blanket was composed of geometric patterns and wide stripes of color that teased the eye.

"Yeah," Helen bit her lip but couldn't hide her smile. "That."

She searched Luciana's face and could sense her angst, her need, and the two of them at war.

"Join me?"

Helen pulled back and sat down on the blanket, kicking her shoes off, and allowing herself to fall backward on the soft, durable fabric.

Luciana shimmied out of her shorts, leaving her body bare in the warm sunlight, then joined Helen on the ground.

"Now I know how you got these," Helen's fingers traced the wounds from The Smiling Man, her voice tinged with sadness. "But…can I ask a strange question?"

"Of course."

"Why don't you have others?"

"I can heal them, if I choose," Luciana propped herself up on an elbow. "I can change any aspect of my appearance, if I choose to."

"So they are a token of respect, of remembrance."

"Yes," Luciana glanced down at her marred stomach. "They are a reminder that I can fail, that I *have* failed."

"I think that's beautiful," Helen put her palm against the largest wound and felt the heat under her skin. "And I think failing is part of living, isn't it?"

"Words of wisdom from a woman who berates herself internally as much as I do," Luciana nudged her gently.

"Ah well, do as I say, not as I do," Helen blew her off with a wave. "All that jazz."

"Well, not something I'm good at doing either, as you've now seen."

"Listen, Luciana, about that."

Her eyebrow rose, but she waited patiently for Helen to continue.

"I can't do that again. I'm so sorry, I-I'm so thankful you showed me but I can't do another vision like that, I–"

"It's ok, you don't have to explain."

"I *want* to," Helen pressed, her voice rising. "I do but–"

"Helen, baby," Luciana's hand reached out and settled gently at Helen's waist. "You don't owe me an explanation."

"I do," Helen pulled back until she could lock eyes with the other woman. "I *do* owe you an explanation."

Luciana opened her mouth to argue, but Helen didn't dare let her, otherwise she might never find the bravery to confess her fears.

"Luciana, I haven't been taking my meds–"

"Helen, I *know*–"

"Please," Helen clenched her hands, defensive anger rising up in her like a serpent coiled in her chest. "Luciana, I need to say this."

"I'm sorry," Luciana shut her mouth, biting her lip to keep from speaking.

"I," Helen rolled onto her stomach, hung her head, and rubbed her temples firmly. "I told you I'd tell you why, that I'd explain it to you when I was ready."

Luciana was clearly wrestling with her desire to respond, but was obediently silent.

"I'm *scared*," Helen choked out after a long moment, finally giving voice to the fear that was rotting her heart. "I'm *terrified* that none of this is real. That you aren't real. That I'm going to snap out of it and…and find myself back on a psych floor somewhere where the doors don't close and people have to watch me take showers."

Helen's whole body was shaking as though she was sitting in an ice bath. Her raw nerves firing nonsense signals and sending pain deep into her chest until she was half-certain she was going into cardiac arrest.

"I–"

Luciana snapped her mouth shut after her single errant syllable, regret plain on her face.

"I know you'll say it is," Helen warded her off. "And honestly, nothing has ever felt *more* real. But it always feels real, until I get lucid, do you understand?"

She searched Luciana's eyes and found nothing but patience.

"May I?"

Helen nodded.

"How can I care best?" she gently reached out and stroked Helen's cheek. "Do you want advice? A listening ear? A distraction?"

"I don't know," Helen could feel her spiral worsening, her heart pounding like a toddler on a new drum at Christmas. "I–"

"You know if you *are nuts*," Helen flinched, but Luciana's soft smile curled her own lip too. "Then that means I'm probably a figment of your imagination, right?"

"Well…"

Hard to argue with that.

"Uh," Helen blinked in confusion. "I guess?"

"So then, basically, if I were to give you advice, that'd just be you giving advice to *yourself*, right?"

"I already do that," Helen snorted, echoing the voice in her head.

"Then ask yourself what difference it makes."

"Sorry?"

"Real, hallucination," Luciana shrugged. "What difference does it make? Are you *happy*? Do you feel safe, do you want–"

"I want this to be real," she blurted out. "I want *you* to be real."

"It is, I am, and you have every right to that happiness."

"But–"

"But what if it isn't?"

"Yeah."

"What *if*?"

"Well, erm."

Helen was at a loss.

"If none of this is real, you've nothing to lose," Luciana inched closer. "But if it *is*, and it's right in front of you. I'm right in front of you."

Helen sealed their conversation with a kiss, and allowed Luciana to roll backward, pulling Helen atop her while their lips remained locked.

"I'll show you something real," Luciana whispered in her ear softly, her breathing heavy as she tugged at the waist of Helen's shorts.

"Yes please," Helen breathed, struggling out of her shorts before resuming her place straddling her lover.

"*This*," Luciana kissed her softly, then snaked one of her hands down between them to cup Helen's vulva. "This is real."

Helen drew a stuttering breath as the woman's fingers spread her lips softly and traced her entrance playfully.

"This pleasure," a finger flickered across her clitoris.

"This frustration," she continued to tease Helen but not enter her.

"This whole, complicated, magical *mess*," Helen trembled as first one, then a second finger slipped inside her. "Is real."

Helen hunched over as Luciana's fingers became more insistent. Her strong, slender digits curled inside of Helen, beckoning her orgasm forward from her very soul. She could feel that she was soaking Luciana's fingers and palm, but her hand was steady as iron as Helen ground against her.

This was a far cry from the frenzied love-making of the station wagon, or the wild, first-kiss sex they'd had back at Casa de Rosas. There was no seduction, no magic, and yet Helen felt more connected to Luciana than ever. She could feel every inch of her fingers, feel the heat from Luciana's own core just inches below her, see the rise and fall of her lover's chest in the sunlight.

The build-up was slow, by comparison, but as the wave of Helen's orgasm finally reached a crest, she cried out, instinctively contracting her muscles and hunching over as waves of pleasure ripped through her.

Her climax was strong enough to wring her muscles out, and she all but collapsed beside Luciana when she was finally able to relax.

"Your turn," she panted past flushed cheeks and a sweaty brow.

"I'm ok," Luciana smiled, pulling Helen close and spooning her in the afternoon sunshine. "I'd rather just have this, if that's ok?"

"Of course," Helen closed her eyes, content with the feeling of Luciana's warm skin against her own.

At some point she must've slept, because when Helen twitched awake some time later, she was alarmed to find it dark outside. She could feel Luciana beside her though, perhaps the only reason she didn't immediately freak out.

"Luciana?"

"Welcome back love."

"How long have I been out?" she stretched, her joints popping but surprisingly pain free after a nap in the middle of a canyon.

"A few hours," she smiled, then rolled onto her back. "Seemed like you needed it."

"I guess I must've," Helen rolled onto her other side, draping her leg and arm over Luciana before setting her head gently against her chest.

They stayed like that for a time. How long, Helen couldn't have said, but she knew one thing for certain—if it never ended, she'd be content.

"Did I ever tell you about the Fae and the stars?"

"Only that they are the source of all magic," she murmured back sleepily.

"That's what some of us believe," Luciana agreed. "That they're the cosmic version of the Fae. Just as we are made of tiny sparks of energy and magic, the stars form the fabric of magic on an even grander scale."

"That's beautiful."

"Maybe it's silly," Helen felt the woman shrug. "But I like to believe that our faith has the ability to make it so, just as human faith shapes Fae existence."

"There's a certain comfort," Helen yawned. "in believing in something larger than yourself."

"Yeah," Helen could hear her smile. "Maybe that's what it is."

"Do Fae believe in the afterlife? In heavens and hells and whatever?"

"Some."

"Some?"

"Many of my kind believe similarly to what human atheists believe," Luciana explained gently. "That when we die, our essence is returned to the great pool of life and magical energy, ready to be reborn into a new form. That there is no 'afterlife' per se, but rather that life continues through our deaths into new living things."

"But you believe something else?"

"I do," Luciana's voice was barely above a whisper. "I have to."

"What do you mean?"

"I mean, I've spent centuries fighting and killing to make the world better, to help people, and I have to believe it was for a reason. If we all just die in the end and nothing has meaning, then what was it all for? What was the point?"

"Maybe life is beautiful *because* it is meaningless," Helen countered, sleepiness making her more willing to blurt out her innermost thoughts. "Maybe pointlessness *is* the point—we're not here for any reason at all, and we try to make it better despite that fact."

Luciana was silent, but Helen could feel the warmth of her quiet even without seeing her facial expression.

"Luciana?"

"Hmm?"

"What did The Smiling Man mean, when he said we couldn't stay here forever?"

She felt the other woman stiffen beneath her.

"When the waystations were first created, they were born of desperation," Luciana answered. "Great wars were fought, violence and destruction on a global scale were not uncommon, and it seemed the only way to build a peace was to create places of neutrality where laws could be crafted, issues could be resolved peacefully, et cetera."

"Ok..."

"But we found a...problem," Luciana sighed heavily. "Our history tells us that the most powerful Fae used the waystations and their neutrality to have unassailable thrones of power, fighting their wars by proxy from within the safety of the sanctuaries."

"Oh."

"So, an agreement was made, the laws were *modified*," Luciana pressed onward. "Now each way station has but one permanent resident—it's caretaker, one of the elders."

"How long do we have?"

"We can stay no longer than one full lunar cycle—twenty nine and a half days."

"Can't we just...step out of the sanctuary and then hop back across the line?"

"No," Luciana laughed softly. "No, the limit is in a given year."

"Ah."

"This is why the elders are sworn to neutrality."

"What happens if they don't stay neutral?"

"Should they ever break their oaths, the deep magic that binds them to these places will shatter, ejecting them from their sanctuary and refusing them entrance at any other. They would be cut off from our most sacred places, and they would forever be vulnerable."

"So, we have four weeks to figure out what we're going to do, then we're out on our asses?"

Another heavy sigh.

"Yes."